Company Wells Fargo

Instructions to Agents and Employés

of the California and Oregon department of Wells, Fargo & Co.'s express,

with tariff of rates, etc

Company Wells Fargo

Instructions to Agents and Employés
of the California and Oregon department of Wells, Fargo & Co.'s express, with tariff
of rates, etc

ISBN/EAN: 9783337784201

Printed in Europe, USA, Canada, Australia, Japan

Cover: Foto ©Andreas Hilbeck / pixelio.de

More available books at **www.hansebooks.com**

INSTRUCTIONS

TO

AGENTS AND EMPLOYÉS

OF

The California and Oregon Department

OF

WELLS, FARGO & CO'S EXPRESS,

WITH

TARIFF OF RATES, ETC.

NOTICE.

This Book of Instructions is designed for the use of the agents and employés of the Express only, and must not be left accessible to the public.

It shall constitute part of the records of an office, and must be transferred by retiring agents and others to their successors.

The Company reserves the right to amend or alter these rules and rates at pleasure.

SAN FRANCISCO:

EXCELSIOR PRESS, BACON & COMPANY, PRINTERS,

536 Clay Street, just below Montgomery.

1868.

CIRCULAR.

To Agents and Employés:

GENTLEMEN: The following Book of Instructions is carefully compiled from the matured experience, written or heretofore unwritten, of those engaged for years in this particular business, and, it is believed, embraces nearly every point upon which a vital question of practice could arise in the routine of an office. It is, moreover, so classified and arranged that any particular subject may readily be referred to, and all necessary light obtained thereon. ·

As such it is commended to your earnest perusal and study, with the assurance that its rules are binding, and that you will be held personally responsible for mistakes originating from a neglect of consulting and obeying them.

Very truly, yours,

CHARLES E. McLANE,

General Agent.

SAN FRANCISCO, Sept. 1st, 1868.

CONTENTS.

GENERAL REMARKS.

THE California and Oregon Express, running over Scope of country embraced. every railroad, stage and steamboat line, extends throughout the States of California, Oregon and Nevada, and territories of Idaho and Washington, and by steamship along the coast to Victoria, V. I., and the principal ports in Mexico. At San Francisco connecting with Wells, Fargo & Co.'s Ocean Expresses for New York, the Atlantic cities, and all parts of Europe —China, Japan and the Sandwich Islands. Also making connection at Salt Lake City with the Overland Express, and at Omaha with United States and American Express Companies for all points in the United States and Canadas.

The Supervision of the California and Oregon Ex- Management. press is under the direct management of JOHN J. VALENTINE, Esq., Superintendent, with headquarters at San Francisco, to whom all questions of detail are to be referred.

The business of the Company consists in forwarding, by rapid modes of conveyance, merchandise, freight, parcels, valuable packages, jewelry, bank-notes, gold, silver, valuable papers, bonds, etc., and delivering the same at the place of business or residence of the consignee; making collections, with or without goods; the filling of orders, and attending to commissions generally.

B

CAUSES OF LOSS AND DISSATISFACTION.

The business is eminently one of detail, requiring of all persons engaged in it, system, accuracy, punctuality, watchfulness, urbanity, *and, above all, that the business of to-day be done before to-morrow.* Among the prolific sources of loss to the Company are :

By goods being improperly *marked.*

By being improperly *packed* for safe carriage.

By carelessness in *handling.*

By receiving goods of little or no value. and forwarding without prepaym nt, and by advancing charges on them.

By carelessness in giving receipts.

By neglecting to notify back when goods are *short.*

By neglecting to carefully check.

By want of uniformity in charges, causing dissatisfaction to the customer.

By want of courtesy and attention to the interests of customers ; thereby injuring the popularity of the Company.

By carelessness in the safe keeping of money and other valuable packages.

By neglecting to adjust promptly all claims for loss or damage.

By neglecting to properly way-bill money packages.

By loss or misplacement of safe, trunk, or treasure-box keys.

By suffering C. O. D. goods to be delivered before payment of bill.

By neglecting to take receipts for goods delivered.

By neglecting to keep watch of money and valuable packages, when in wagons or coaches.

To obviate these evils, and to insure uniformity in each department throughout the entire business, a strict observance of the following rules is enjoined upon all the employés of the Company.

GENERAL INSTRUCTIONS.

NOTE.—In the compilation of these instructions, it is proper to state, the utmost freedom has been exercised in drawing from books of this kind already published, and particularly from that of THE OVERLAND EXPRESS, OR SALT LAKE DEPARTMENT OF WELLS, FARGO & Co., which has been found very complete and applicable to the system adopted.

PERSONAL CONDUCT.

1. All persons connected with the business of the Company are expected to deport themselves with uniform civility and affability, and to answer all questions of business addressed to them, in a clear, and, as far as possible, satisfactory manner. *Civility to Customers.*

2. Clerks, drivers. and messengers will be subject to the direction and instruction of the agent at the office where employed, or where their duties may require them temporarily to remain. *Authority over clerks and messengers.*

3. For the more direct communication with and complete supervision of, the various offices under his control, the Superintendent will appoint and employ assistants, to be known as traveling agents, who will from time to time visit the offices, and whose orders and instructions, in all matters pertaining to the business of the same, are to be carefully observed. *Authority of traveling agents over offices.*

4. When good cause is given, agents will suspend from duty messengers, running from, or any person *Agents may suspend employés for misconduct.*

employed in, their office, and consult the Superintendent as to further action.

Misconduct to be reported to traveling agent.

5. Any gross misconduct on the part of messengers, such as drinking intoxicating liquors while on duty, carrying money packages past way-stations, leaving their safes unguarded, etc., must be reported to the traveling agent or Superintendent; and any employé who may be cognizant of default in duty by another employé and fails to report the same to the traveling agent of his division, or Superintendent, becomes equally censurable with the defaulter.

Employés responsible for damages.

6. When the Company meets with a loss through the carelessness, inattention, or want of prudence of agents or messengers, they will be held personally responsible for such loss, or such proportion thereof as the traveling agent may determine.

Leave of absence.

7. Agents exclusively engaged to attend to the Company's business will not absent themselves from the same without permission from the proper authority. No office should be left a moment unless in charge of a regular watch, or some responsible person in the employ of the Company.

CARE OF OFFICES AND PROPERTY.

All business strictly confidential.

8. The business of the Company, and the transactions of its customers through its offices, must be strictly confidential, and books, bills, etc., *are not* open for public inspection.

Intrusion prohibited.

9. No person shall be allowed behind the counters except the employés of the Company having business there; and when receiving or forwarding treasure, no person shall be permitted within reach of it, unless his duties or responsibilities are connected with the same.

Secrecy to be observed.

10. Information concerning the amount of money received or forwarded, or in relation to any matter of business intrusted to the Company, must not be given to any one. Secrecy is the main guard and protection of all express business.

11. Safes, treasure-boxes, and keys, in offices or otherwise used, must at all times be kept where they are inaccessible to persons not employed by the Company, and whose business does not pertain to them. *Keys, treasure-boxes etc., to be kept secure.*

12. Agents, on routes where no messengers are employed, must take the treasure-box to a *private and safe place*, and there check its contents, being particular that no one else may acquaint himself with the contents of the box or way-bills. *Opening treasure box en route.*

13. The lock of a safe, or treasure-box, must always be tried after the key is taken out, to be *certain* that it is locked, and the key must be kept in a secure place. *Precaution to insure its being locked.*

14. Losing a key or sending off a treasure-box without being locked, will be considered gross neglect of duty, and be held as sufficient cause for dismissal and being disqualified from ever after returning to the service. *Penalty for loss of key or sending box unlocked.*

RECEIVING AND DELIVERING GOODS.
CHECKING WAY-BILLS.

15. Upon the arrival of the express at an office, and the receipt of goods and way-bills, the agent, or his assistant, will, at once, ascertain, by careful comparison, if the goods called for on way-bill have been received, and for each article thus received he will place his initial as a check-mark to the entry on way-bill corresponding therewith, and if anything is short, note the fact in writing opposite such entry. The several entries on the way-bill must then be transferred to the delivery book, and proper efforts made for the prompt delivery of goods to parties addressed. *Noting on way-bills when goods fail to arrive.* *Delivery-book.*

RECEIPTS.

16. Agents will take receipts in " delivery receipt book," for all goods, etc., delivered, and will, in *all cases*, require freight and charges to be paid on delivery, except in cases of season contracts, (S. C.) *Charges must be paid on or before delivery.*

17. When the consignee of a valuable package is *Identification of consignees.*

Signature for identification.

unknown, *he must be identified* by some responsible person, (the presentation of the Company's receipt is not sufficient) and the person identifying *must sign with party receiving*, upon the receipt-book; and all receipts must be taken under the date on which the package is delivered.

Orders for delivery to be preserved.

18. When packages are delivered upon written order of party to whom they are addressed, the order must be preserved by pasting the same in back of receipt-book upon which the article is receipted.

Agents responsible for proper delivery.

19. Agents will be held personally responsible for the freight and charges on goods delivered at their respective offices, or the wrong delivery of any package.

Goods addressed to "care of."

20. Goods or articles addressed to the "care of" an individual or company, *must be delivered to that individual or company*, and not to the person to whom addressed.

Transferring to "Old Horse," and notifying consignees.

21. All goods not called for within twenty-four hours after being received, should be transferred to the "Old Horse" or "package-on-hand" book furnished for that purpose, and consignee notified through the post-office, with the usual blanks. Every exertion should be made to deliver packages, and not allow them to accumulate.

NOTIFYING SHORT PACKAGES.

Prompt measures to trace them.

22. In every instance of goods failing to arrive with the way-bills referring to same, immediate and energetic steps must be taken to trace and find them. The agent will write the office from which the missing article started, also the last intermediate checking-office, and notify messenger, if there is one.

Short money packages to be notified by telegraph.

23. When money packages are short or missing, he will telegraph and write immediately, same as above.

Records of way-bills passing, for reference.

24. Agents must keep such records of goods and way-bills passing through their offices as will enable them to be traced. Offices must be prepared, in way above indicated, to give the *time* the delayed goods passed through their hands.

25. Every agent failing to notify, at once, when goods are short, will be held as having received them.

Penalty for neglect.

CLAIMS FOR DAMAGES.

26. When damages are claimed, the agent should personally examine into the claim, and not refer it to employés.

Personal examination by agents.

27. When claim for damages exceeds $10, it must be referred to the traveling agent or Superintendent, and instructions asked.

Reference to traveling agent and Superintendent.

28. If suits are brought against the Company, the traveling agent, and the Superintendent at San Francisco, must be immediately notified.

Suits for damages.

"OFFING" CHARGES.

29. When a package is received, the charges on which, by reason of being in excess of schedule rate, or for other good and sufficient reasons, are calculated to give serious dissatisfaction to consignee, agents may "off" in remarks column such amount as may be deemed necessary, provided such amount does not affect the column of "advanced charges;" and under no circumstances shall charges reported as "advanced" be deducted either in whole or in part.

Limitation of this privilege.

Advanced charges cannot be "offed."

30. In judging whether an actual overcharge has been made, when such is alleged to be the case, agents will consult the Company's own figures, and not be influenced by the amount paid to connecting lines and appearing as "advanced charges."

How a question of overcharge must be determined.

31. When a package is entered free on a way-bill the address of the consignee must be given. When a package is entered on way-bills to collect, and the agent delivering it "offs" or excuses payment of the same, he must always state explicitly on the way-bill the reason for such action.

Reason for sending or delivering packages free to be stated.

MARKING AND PACKING.

MARKING FREIGHT.

32. As the cause of many errors and complaints is found in defective marking and packing, agents and others employed in receiving and forwarding goods, will make these points a matter of very serious attention.

Address to be conspicuous. 33 The address on articles of freight and boxes must, in all cases, be plainly and conspicuously marked thereon, and whenever possible, with *marking paint*.

Office labels. 34. The printed label of the Company, giving the name of the office at which such article is received and billed, must also be attached on the same side with the address.

MONEY PACKAGES.

Money packages to be sealed. 35. In all cases money packages must be securely sealed with the private seal of the shipper or that of Wells, Fargo & Co. But in no case must the latter be used unless the agent knows the value of contents.

Precaution in receipting. 36. The exact amount of money contained in packages must be plainly marked on them, and no money package be *receipted* for until after it is sealed.

Manner of sealing the envelope. 37. Every currency package put up in an envelope must have five seals upon it, as follows; one on the centre, and one on each seam of the envelope, half-way from the centre to the corner, as shown in the diagram below.

Sealing large packages. 38. No package of money in an envelope must be allowed to leave an office without being thus sealed.

Large packages of money, otherwise put up, must be so securely sealed that they can by no possibility be tampered with without detection.

39. If any error or short count occurs in packages not sealed in accordance with these instructions, the amount will be charged back to the agent or office forwarding the same. *Penalty for neglecting these particulars.*

40. Gold-dust should be put in strong and well-sewed buckskin bags, tied, and well sealed. Tin cans must not be used, as the least jar breaks the solder on the seams, and it sifts out. *Packing of gold-dust.*

41. Shippers should avoid, as much as possible, the practice of putting more than one gold bar in a package. They are liable to break the packing and obliterate the mark. When bars or coin are put up in boxes, the lid should be *screwed* on, and the screw-heads sealed with wax. *Packing bars or coin.*

TAGS AND LABELS.

42. In all cases where it is found that the address on packages, etc., is liable to be obliterated or chafed off in the course of a long journey, agents must attach to such package the stout address-tag furnished for that purpose, and plainly write the address thereon. *Durable tags to be substituted for frail ones.*

43. Second only to the imperfect and careless marking of address upon a box or package as a source of error and confusion, is the neglect of putting the usual office label thereon. Agents are specially directed to guard against this neglect. In all cases, the label must show the name of the office from which it is sent. (if not printed, it must be written) and the label must be put on the same side of the box or package, or way-billed letter. with the address, so that it will be impossible to overlook it. *Office labels. Importance and manner of their use.*

44. The inconsiderate practice of attaching the label to the back of a letter or other package, or otherwise out of immediate observation, is seriously reprehended. *Improper use.*

C

45. This rule applies to *all* matter upon which the name of billing office does not otherwise appear.

C. O. D. labels.

46. In C. O. D. packages, etc., care must be taken to attach the " C. O. D." label, as the neglect of so doing may occasion error in the treatment of such packages, etc., for which the agent causing the error will be held personally liable.

Supply to be prepared for use.

47. Agents who are not furnished with labels having the office name printed thereon, will consult their own convenience and expedite business by making and keeping a *written* supply on hand.

RECEIVING GOODS TO BE FORWARDED.

RECEIPTS.

Receipts to be given.

48. A receipt must be given to the sender for every package to be forwarded, valuable or otherwise, and all valuable packages locked in the safe until checked out and sent forward.

Value to be put on all packages.

49. Agents must require a value to be put on every package by the shipper, which value he will insert in the receipt. It is not necessary to way-bill such value in all cases. It is required to enable the Company more readily to settle damages in case of loss.

Receipts for packages to way-stations, and beyond routes.

50. Money and other packages must not be received for places on our routes where we have no office or no certain arrangements for their delivery. If the place is off our routes, the receipt given must specify " to be delivered to connecting express."

MAKING CHARGES.

A price to be put on each article.

51. A price should be put on every package billed, unless it is a " free," " P. O. R.," or " S. C." package ; if wrong, the office receiving can add to, or deduct from the charge, by using the column provided in the way-bill and statement for that purpose ; but a price is

Price to be based on knowledge of package.

never to be made for forwarding an article without the agent seeing and knowing something of its weight, bulk, contents, and value.

52. A general tariff is furnished to each office, and must not be varied from except by consent of the Superintendent. *Tariff to be followed.*

53. When entirely in doubt about the charge to be made on packages, or when contract is for office at destination to fix the price, the agent may enter it M. P., (make price) and the agent receiving will then fix the charge, and *add* to the bill in column of remarks, which will be taken upon statement sheet in " add " column. *Cases of extreme doubt as to charge.*

54. In no case is one agent to alter charges made by another agent, except in this way, as the original footing of a bill must never be altered, by the change of a figure or the introduction of any new figures into the charges columns. *Changes from original entry to be made in remarks column.*

55. Shippers are required to put a value on every article, and agents to so book it, and enter it in receipt and on way-bill. This valuation must influence, in a measure, the charges made.

56. Agents must exercise great care in making *special agreements* and always consult authority. All *contracts*, made by one agent, are to be faithfully fulfilled by any other agent, whenever a *receipt*, with an agreement on it, or other *good evidence*, is shown. When contracts are not in accordance with the tariff, the *receipt* should be taken from the holder and sent to the Superintendent. *Special contracts.*

57. Express matter forwarded under monthly or season contracts, bears no charge on way-bill. " S. C." must be put in column of remarks. *Forwarding S. C. goods.*

FRAGILE, WORTHLESS AND PERISHABLE GOODS.

58. Goods evidently not worth the transportation, or that would not, under ordinary circumstances, sell for the charges, *must not be received* unless the charges are *prepaid* or guaranteed. When freight is prepaid, the person receiving the money will mark the package " paid," with his name or initials. *Goods of uncertain value to be prepaid or guaranteed.*

Care in advancing charges.

59. Especial care must be taken, in advancing charges on goods, to know that they are worth charges and freight.

Nature of contents to be shown and goods taken at shipper's risk only.

60. All packages containing poultry, fish, fruit, or perishable articles of any description, or articles contained in glass, should have their nature distinctly marked upon them, as also the full address of the consignee, including street and number, *and must only be received at owner's risk, and charges must be prepaid to destination.*

Duplicate receipts with written acquiescence to be taken.

61. These conditions must be specified in the receipt, and in order to have such contract for reference, in case of loss or damage, agents will give a receipt, and require a *duplicate*, with agreement and signature of shipper across face of same, assuming and agreeing to considerations given therein. A five-cent revenue

Rev. Stamp.

stamp must be attached to such contract, to make it legally binding.

SALE OF PERISHABLE GOODS, IF REFUSED.

Judicious persons to be consulted.

62. When perishable goods are refused by consignee, or not called for, (unless other instructions accompany them) they should at once be disposed of to the best advantage, after having consulted some judicious person in the trade, as to the manner and propriety of so

Account of sale to be rendered.

doing, and an account of sales, with net proceeds, returned to the shipper, addressed to the office from which the goods came. If the shipper is not known, the account of sales may be sent to the agent where shipped from, and he will ascertain who is entitled to the proceeds.

THE OVERLAND EXPRESS.

Scope and Territory.

63. This department of the Company's business commences at Omaha, Nebraska, along the route of the Union Pacific Railroad, and by stage to Salt Lake City; thence north, through Virginia City and Helena to Fort Benton in Montana, and to Boise City in Idaho. Connections are made at Omaha with the

United States and American Express Companies for all points in the United States and Canada. Also connecting at Cheyenne with the United States Express Company for principal points in Colorado and New Mexico. The headquarters of this department are at Salt Lake City.

64. To shippers wishing to save time, the Overland Express offers superior advantages. for points in the Atlantic States, for packages, parcels and treasure. The rapid construction of the great National Highway —the Pacific Railroad—gives this route an importance not hitherto considered. A year or eighteen months will give a railroad communication between the Eastern and Pacific States, when the express charges will be materially lessened, and the time greatly shortened. *Advantages to shippers.*

65. Agents will bill to Salt Lake City all matter for points east of there, intended to go overland, and for points in Montana; and when charges are to collect, the amount given should be the proper rate to Salt Lake City, and not to destination. *Where to bill and how.*

66. Prepayment of charges to destination may be received, but in all cases of prepayment, agents must note in "remarks" column, "paid to S. L. C," or "paid through," as the case may be. *Prepaid charges.*

WAY BILLS—NUMBERING, ETC.

67. Particular care is to be taken that no express is forwarded without the proper way-bills accompanying it. *Way bills must accompany goods.*

68. All bills made and forwarded in any one day, at the same office, must bear the same number; therefore, bills sent by any *one* office to another office, will not bear consecutive numbers, unless it happen that a bill is sent to that particular office each day. *All way-bills of same date to bear same number.*

69. On the first of January of each year, agents will commence their way-bills with number one, and keep on numbering without regard to dates, advancing a number every day that one or more bills are forwarded. *Number 1 to begin the first day of each year.*

(Form of Entries on a Way-Bill.)

Way-Bill, No. 245.

WELLS, FARGO & CO.'S EXPRESS.

E. V. THORN, Messenger. Sept. 1, 1868. From SAN JOSE to SAN FRANCISCO.

ARTICLES.	Amount	From whom received.	To whom addressed.	Destination.	Advanced Charges.	Our Charges	Prepaid.	Collect	Remarks.
1 Paid C. O. D. & Coin...	38	E. Reed...	Bacon & Company.	San Francisco..		2 50		2 50	
2 Trunks...		Auzerais House...	T. Parrott.	Do.		1 00		1 00	Free.
Pkg. C. O. D...	38	W. G. Roberts...	S. Allen & Co.	Do.		50		50	
Coin...	85	J. O. Brown...	W. H. Harvey...	De.					
Parcel, V...	100	A. Edwards...	J. C. Johnson...	Philadelphia...					Contract, $3.50 through.
Com'n...		Jno. Edwards...	W., F. & Co...	San Francisco.		50	50	50	P. O. K.
Box and Pkg...			{W.H. Smith care} {Cosmop. Hotel.}	Do.					
3 Sid. Bags...	10000	Knox & B...	Bank of California.	Do.		2 00		2 00	Guaranteed.
1 Bbl. (Apples)...		Dewitt & Co...	Drake & Emerson.	Do.		12 50	12 50		Paid through.
1 Trunk and Valise...		Howard...	S. Girard.	New York...		15 00	15 00		Returned free.
Comm. and Coin...	185	Jones & Co...	W., F. & Co...	San Francisco..		3 00	3 00		
1 Letter Currency...	300	W. F. B...	Alsop & Co...	Do.		1 00		1 50	
Ret'd Coll'n...	450	Jones & Co...	Knox & Beans...	Do.	3 50			4 50	Protested.
Statement and Coin...	$7650	Agt...	Cashr. Inter. Exp.	Do.		1 00			Free.
1 Pkg...		S. Clara...	W. G. Henry...	Do.					
20 Boxes, (Apple)...		Jewett & Co...	Washington Market	Do.	50	60		1 00	
3 Bales and Bedstead...		W. H. English...	W. H. English...	Do.		10 00		10 00	M. P.
1 Pkg...		E. Reed, Agent...	West. Un. Tol. Co.	Do.					S. C.

(Form of Entries on a Way-Bill.)

Way-Bill, No. 245.

WELLS, FARGO & CO.'S EXPRESS.

E. G. KELTON, Messenger.   Sept. 1st, 1868.   From SAN FRANCISCO to SALT LAKE CITY.

Articles.	Amount.	From whom received.	To whom addressed.	Destination.	Advanced Charges.	Our Charges.	Prepaid.	Collect.	Remarks.
1 Box....		Treadwell & Co....	T. B. H. Stenhouse.	Salt Lake City		5 20		5 20	13 lbs.
1 Fd. Com. and Saw....	80	W., F. & Co....	R. Young....	Do.		16 00		16 00	37 lbs.
Parcel Coin....		J. Howard....	W. G. Henry....	Do.		3 00	3 00		Paid through.
1 Pkg....		J. Stewart....	Armstrong & Co....	Memphis, Tenn.		6 00	6 00		103 lbs.
1 Bale....		Murphy, G. & Co....	Wm. Jennings....	Salt Lake City.		41 20		41 20	P. O. R.
1 Com'n....		Lloyd & Sharp....	W., F. & Co....	Do.		400 00		400 00	Contract thro', $700.
1 Pkg. Currency Val.	20000	W., F. & Co....	Husey, Dahler & Co	Va. City, M. T.		300 00	300 00		
3 Sld. Bags....	15000	Do.	B'g Dpt. W. F. & Co	Salt Lake City		37 50		37 50	Guaranteed.
4 Boxes....		Meagher, T. & Co....	Eldridge & Clawson	Do.		26 50		26 50	Do.
5 Boxes Oranges....		Washington Market	A. Gaisford....	Do.		7 25		7 25	Do.
1 Roll Blankets....		Jo. S. Roberson	Elder Robert Sands	Do.		4 50		4 50	Do.
1 Box....		Kaeding & Co....	W. A. Gillespie....	Omaha....		8 25	8 20		Contract thro', $8.
Coin Parcel....	275	Jno. Jones....	Thomas Henry....	Chicago....		18 00		18 00	Paid through.
1 Box....		L. Wines....	T. F. Wood....	New York....		5 00			Contract thro', $40.
Coin....	100	Jo. Jones....	C. C. Pendergast....	Concord, N. H.		5 00	5 00		Paid through.
Parcel Currency....	500	Bank of California.	Quigly, Lyons & Co.	Louisville, Ky.		22 50	22 50		Do.
1 Pkg....		C. E. McI., Gen. Ag	Jos. J. Younglove....	Bowl'g Gr', Ky.		4 50	4 50		Do.

Where to bill to. Billing beyond regular routes.

70. For any point off our lines, agents billing will only make way bills and charges to the office to which they are authorized to bill.

Entry of prepaid through charges.

71. But, if the charges are prepaid to destination, the full amount paid is to be extended in column of "our charges," and in "prepaid column," adding in column of "remarks," "*paid through*." The office that receives such package will rebill it without charge, saying, "Paid through on —— Bill," giving date and name of office issuing the bill.

Collect charges agreed through.

72. When charges are to collect, and rate has been agreed through, the charges should be entered only to point billed to, and the price agreed upon to destination noted in column of remarks.

Name of consignor.

73. Agents will always enter on way-bill, in column "from whom received," the name of the party who delivers packages or goods to them.

Goods sent under private mark.

74. When goods are received and to be forwarded, marked with a private mark, or an initial letter, the name of consignee must in all cases be ascertained, and entered with that of consignor, in full, upon the way-bill, with destination.

Registers of way-bills received and sent.

75. Correct copies of all bills forwarded must be kept in a book furnished for that purpose, and those received in another book of the kind required.

Messengers to check.

76. Agents will require *out* messengers to check every entry on their bills with initials of name.

Folding way-bills.

77. Agents will be particular to fold the largest size of way-bills by first turning them over lengthwise, into the size of smaller ones, and then transversely.

MEMORANDUM WAY-BILLS.

Mem. way-bills from regular offices when admissible.

78. No package shall be forwarded unless accompanied by a regular or memorandum way-bill, to guide and govern agents through whose hands it must pass. At all offices a regular way-bill, duly numbered and registered, must be sent forward with all packages. The only exception allowable is when forwarding a

package after the final disposition of the regular way-bill has been made, (such as noting it on abstract or delivery to messenger) in which case a memorandum bill must be sent.

79. When a package becomes detached or separated, *en route*, from its way-bill, agents discovering same in the process of checking other bills, will at once make out a memorandum way-bill, noting thereon addresses, destination, and other essential particulars of which they may be cognizant. and forward same, duly checked, with such package.

Mem. way-bills to be forwarded with estray packages.

80. When, afterward, the regular way-bill happens to arrive, the agent making the memorandum bill, or, in case of his neglect, any agent acquainted with the preceding facts, will note on the regular way-bill, in remarks column, "Hence," and will omit placing his check-mark thereon.

Marking "Ahead."

81. Agents making memorandum way-bills, must preserve a record of the same, giving all requisite particulars and the date of forwarding such bills, which record may be canceled when regular way-bill is known to have gone forward.

Record of mem. way-bills.

82. It occurs more frequently that a regular way-bill becomes separated from its packages and goes forward in advance of them. In such cases, agents will mark all such entries "Short," and preserve a record thereof. See paragraphs 22, 25, pp. 14, 15. The same entry afterward appearing on a memorandum bill with the package, must have noted thereon, if not so noted already, "Reg. W. B. hence."

Marking regular bills for short packages.

83. No way-bill entry shall be checked by any agent with his initial, unless the thing called for is actually within his observation and control, either on hand or in transitu.

Precaution in checking.

84. Memorandum way-bills must not be entered on the regular way-bill registers, nor be accounted for on abstracts or statements.

Mem. bills not to be accounted for.

D

CUSTODY AND HANDLING OF FREIGHT.

Injury to be prevented. 85. All employés handling freight are required to do their duty with such thoughtful care, that the frailest article may be forwarded with the certainty of being delivered entire and uninjured. To effect this, it is necessary that no article, of whatever description, be thrown, dropped, or allowed to fall, no matter how short the distance.

Disposition frail packages in transitu. 86. Nor shall it be allowed that packages, etc., evidently of frail character, shall be thoughtlessly or willfully so disposed of, along with stouter packages and freight, as to cause them to be crushed and broken.

Neglect to be inexcusable. 87. A neglect of ordinary precaution in this particular, which has been heretofore of frequent occurrence, will not be tolerated in future, if the guilty can possibly be detected.

Precautionary requests to be carefully heeded 88. Boxes and other packages upon which is marked "This side up," "Keep dry," "Handle with care," or with any precautionary request whatsoever, shall be handled and disposed of accordingly, to the utmost ability of those having charge thereof.

Goods not to be left unguarded. 89. When the messenger has occasion to leave the car or coach at a station, as for meals, the agent at such station will either remain in charge of his express, or substitute a suitable person to watch over it during the messenger's absence; and in all such cases, the **Messengers not allowed to relinquish their keys.** messenger will make it his especial care to lock the safe, treasure-boxes, or trunks containing valuable packages, before absenting himself, and to take the keys with him.

DELIVERING GOODS WITH WAGONS.

Goods to be kept secure. 90. In carrying for delivery, money packages and specie on our wagons, they must be kept in a safe or trunk, locked, and *constantly in sight.*

Identification. 91. The person delivering such packages must require the satisfactory identification of parties addressed, (when personally unknown to him) in writing, along with the signature receipting for same on his delivery-book.

92. Receipts must be taken for *all* articles thus de-livered. Receipts.

COLLECTION AND COMMISSION DE-PARTMENT.

NATURE OF COLLECTIONS.

93. There is no branch, perhaps, of the business of the Express, in which the genius and tact of an agent can be so forcibly and advantageously exerted, as in that relating to the successful collection of money, and its prompt and satisfactory return to the proper owner. *Importance of this branch.*

94. In entering upon the general instructions relating to this branch, particular attention is invited to the material difference of meaning conveyed in the various descriptive terms applied to collections—a difference which, if overlooked, may occasion difficulty, confusion, and sometimes loss. Thus, collections, when first for-warded, are treated simply as " Collections ;" when re-turned paid, as " Paid Collections ;" when returned *not* paid, as " Returned Collections." *Descriptive terms in use.*

95. A C. O. D. (collect on delivery) is a distinct va-riety of collection. This mark always means that there is something else to be collected on goods besides the charges, before they are delivered—the cost of purchase, for example—and the goods must not be opened or de-livered until the collection is paid. The shipper's in-structions leave us no discretion in this matter. *Nature of C.O.D. collection.*

96. A " Collection " may consist of a check, draft, note, due-bill, or other evidence of indebtedness, which is sent forward to be presented to the debtor for pay-ment, but is usually unaccompanied by any other matter except the instructions of the agent forwarding, and which must, in all cases, govern the actions of the agent making the collection. *Nature of collec-tion proper.* *Instructions to be obeyed.*

TREATMENT OF COLLECTIONS.

Use of proper envelopes.

97. When drafts, notes, or bills are taken for collection, the Company's collection receipt must always be given, and the draft, note, or bill, inclosed in the proper collection envelope.

Signatures to be certified.

98. When a note or draft is drawn to the order of the party sending it for collection, agents must not fail to procure the signature or indorsement of such person on the back of such paper, before forwarding it, and must certify beneath that the signature of indorser is genuine. Much delay and loss is caused by a neglect of this important rule.

Non-payment to be promptly reported.

99. Where collections are due at sight, or on demand, and not paid on presentation, whether ordered protested, or not to be protested, the office sending must be immediately notified of the fact. And wherever delay occurs from absence of parties, or other cause, advice of the fact must be immediately returned.

Importance of so doing.

100. This is vitally important; and the merchant and public generally who intrust their business to the company are ever anxious for information in case of delay. Forms for advice, which are simple, and generally require but few words, are furnished each office.

Collections to be returned if not paid.

101. As a general rule, where collections are not promptly paid, they should be returned; but where an agent deems it advisable to hold for a short time, the fact must be advised.

Correspondence in relation to collections.

102. Any advice or correspondence in regard to collections must be addressed to the office sending them, and in *no instance* to the parties from whom they are received. Any deviation from this only tends to delay and confusion.

Money to be taken in payment.

103. Sound discretion should be used with regard to the kind of money taken on collections. The custom of the place where the collection is made determines the kind of money in which it is to be paid, unless the face of the paper specifies it. As far as possible, the money

best suited to the party for whom the collection is made,
should be collected.

104. When instructions are given to return proceeds
of collection by draft, the draft must be made payable
to the order of the party in whose favor the collection
is made. *Never to the order of the Express Company.*

Manner of drawing drafts used in payment.

COLLECTIONS ORDERED PROTESTED.

105. Too much care cannot be exercised in receiving
collections liable to protest for non-acceptance or non-
payment, as herein the company incurs a direct pecu-
niary responsibility. To protest a paper is to transfer
it, after failing to procure acceptance or payment, to
the hands of a notary public, or other officer having
legal authority, who will present the same for acceptance or payment, and in default thereof, will, in his
official capacity, attach a written protest to such paper,
and at once notify the drawer and indorser, or indorsers,
that the same has been protested, and that holders look
to them for payment.

Nature of a protest.

106. Agents are authorized to pay the usual fee for
this service, and report same, in return of protested
collection, as " advanced charges."

Notary's fee.

107. The agent receiving a collection should ascertain the wish of the party, in regard to protesting, and
give receipt in accordance—and note instructions carefully on the envelope.

Wishes of sender to be consulted.

108. He should procure in all cases the residence of
drawers of drafts, and indorsers of notes, and write same
under the name of such drawer or indorser.

Residences of drawers and indorsers.

109. When acceptance of time-drafts is procured,
and the same are not paid at maturity, they must in all
cases be protested for non-payment.

Protest for non-payment of accepted drafts.

110. When a time draft has been presented for acceptance, and the same declined, it must be protested
for such *non-acceptance,* and held until maturity, and
again presented, this time for payment, in default of

Protest for non-acceptance and for non-payment.

Expenses and charges.

which, it must again be protested for non-payment, and then return to office from whence it came, agent making proper charges in "Our charges" column, for trouble and the return of collection, and billing as "Advanced charges" the expenses incurred for protests. Special attention is directed to this peculiarity in treatment of time drafts.

Special Instructions to be obeyed.

111. Any special instructions written on the envelope, conflicting with the above, must, however, be strictly adhered to. For further information of agents in making collections of this character, the following remarks are subjoined.

ACCEPTANCE OF A BILL OR DRAFT.

Form of an acceptance.

112. An acceptance is an engagament to pay a bill or draft, and is done by the drawee (the person on whom the draft is made) writing "accepted" across the face of the paper, and subscribing his name; and when a specified time of payment is mentioned, (as ten days after sight) the drawee should date the time of acceptance.

Consequences of failure to protest.

113. When, in case of time drafts, instructions are to protest, which must be for non-acceptance and non-payment, and it is not accepted or paid, it must be twice protested as indicated above, or the drawee and indorsers are discharged from liability.

Necessity of protesting on day when due.

114. A draft must be presented for payment, and properly protested on the day it becomes due, or the Express Company will be held liable for its payment, and the indorser exonerated. Even the bankruptcy, insolvency, or death of the acceptor, (or drawee) will

No contingency whatever serving as an excuse.

not excuse a neglect to demand payment of the assignees or executors, nor will the insufficiency of a draft or note, in any respect, constitute an excuse, so far as the Company is concerned, for non-payment.

Time and place of presentation.

115. The presentment should be made at a reasonable time of day, when the bill is due. If the paper is

made payable at any specified place, it must be presented at such place for payment.

116. If a draft or note falls due on Sunday or any public holiday, and if such holiday fall on Monday, the paper becomes due on Saturday, except in States, where, by law, it becomes due the day after Sunday or holiday. *Rule in relation to Sundays and public holidays.*

117. When any doubt arises as to the proper course to be pursued in making a collection, agents should always consult a lawyer or bank officer, or some one competent to advise, and in all cases the agent should acquaint himself with the statutes bearing on this subject in the locality where he resides. *Authorities to be consulted in case of doubt.*

118. Agents must avoid, in all cases, receiving any amount on account of a collection unless the whole is paid —except when special instructions are given to do so; in such cases, the amount must be remitted to the office sending, with particular advice. *Part-payments to be refused unless otherwise instructed.*

119. When coin is remitted for paid collections, it should be put up in a separate package, sealed and distinctly marked, referring to the number on the envelope. No coin must be sealed and forwarded in the collection envelope. *Coin remittances in payment.*

120. Agents are required to re-bill returned or paid collections to the office from whence they were billed, and all answers to inquirers in relation to outstanding collections must be returned in the same way. *How to return collections and correspondence.*

121. A book is furnished each regular office in which all collections made or forwarded must be entered, as per form therein. *Collection register.*

C. O. D. COLLECTIONS.

122. When bills are taken, accompanying goods to be collected on delivery of same, they must be inclosed in the printed "C. O. D." envelope for that purpose, and marked plainly "C. O. D." on the package, and also the amount of bill to be collected, and a "C. O. D." label attached. *Treatment of C. O. D. bills and packages.*

Charges to embrace return of money. 123. Enough charges must be made on the goods to pay for making the collection and returning the money, and the funds are to be returned accordingly, free of further charge.

Part payment. 124. A portion of the bill must not be collected on the delivery of a portion of the goods, unless by special instructions, in writing, from the shipper.

Short Advices. 125. When "C. O. D." goods arrive in advance of, or without the collection, the office from whence they were sent must immediately be notified, giving the name of consignee and consignor, if known.

*Discretion of Agents. 126. If the agent is satisfied of the proper amount to be collected, he may deliver the goods, on payment of same, and remit to the office from whence goods were received, giving such information as will enable the agent at that point to deliver the money to the proper owner.

Delays to be reported. 127. Where, in the case of C. O. D.'s unusual delay occurs in parties not taking their goods, advice of the same, with cause, should be returned.

Reporting C. O. D. to General Office. 128. When any C. O. D. package has been on hand one month, the agent must report it to the Superintendent at San Francisco with advice, unless he has official instructions to retain it a longer time.

TRANSFERRING COLLECTIONS TO CONNECTING EXPRESSES.

Collections to be reënveloped. 129. In order to insure the return of all collections passing out of the Company's hands, to other companies, and also that agents may have less trouble in keeping their accounts of such business, agents at transfer offices will, in each and every instance, *reënvelope all collections transferred to other companies, retaining the original envelope in their possession*, until the return of collection.

Transferring instructions. 130. In filling out the new envelope, it must be made out in favor of "Wells, Fargo & Co.," at the office where transferred, and particular attention must be paid to enter thereon all special or general instructions, given on the original envelope.

131. When such collections are returned, they must be inclosed in the original envelope, *without breaking the seal of the company returning it*, and again be sealed with the official seal in the usual way.

How reinclosed in original envelope.

COMMISSIONS.

132. The most popular feature of an Express, is that it furnishes a reliable, speedy, and responsible medium for the transaction of all kinds of business at places more or less remote from each other ; and in furtherance of this design, every encouragement is to be given to its use for the purpose of making special purchases, and for attending to other matters of commission.

Special purchases.

133. All orders for purchase of goods, or articles of any kind, must be forwarded in "Commission Envelopes," and be accompanied by cash sufficient to cover the full estimated amount of purchase. In all cases where this rule is not observed, the agent sending the commission will be held personally responsible for the money expended, or the commission will be returned unattended to.

Commission envelopes to be used.

Cash to accompany the orders.

134. In general, commissions must be addressed to "Agent Wells, Fargo & Co.," etc.

LETTER DEPARTMENT.

135. Agents will endeavor to build up this branch of the business, by promptness in the delivery of letters, and care and dispatch in forwarding them. Every exertion must be made to find the place of business or residence, if unknown, of persons addressed, and as soon as letters are received, a messenger, where there is one, should be sent to deliver them.

Care and dispatch.

136. If parties cannot be found, a list of the letters remaining in an office must be kept in some conspicuous place.

List of letters on hand.

E

Requisition for franks.

137. FRANKS (or pre-paid government envelopes) must be ordered from Cashier Express Department, San Francisco, in sufficient time to get them before previous supply is exhausted. They will be sent billed as "advanced charges" for the amount of their value.

"OLD HORSE," OR PACKAGES ON HAND.

All charges accounted for.

138. Agents must account to the general office in their statements for the charges of every package received, whether delivered or not.

Annual reports to General Office.

139. At the end of each year a list of all packages, either money, parcels, or goods, that have accumulated during the year, must be returned to San Francisco Office under the head of "Old Horse," giving address of package, when received, where from, and amount of charges due; a copy so returned must be kept in the office sending.

Disposition of O. H. in statement.

140. Earnest and persistent efforts must be made by an agent to deliver all packages received. If, however, any remain on hand at the end of the month, with charges, agents can use such funds as they may take in on the "Out" business between first of month and the time that the statement is rendered, to make it good with Cashier.

SETTLING WITH GENERAL OFFICE.

GENERAL REMARKS.

The abstract and the statement.

141. Two separate reports and settlements of the business of an office are required to be made each month, the one to embrace the contents of way-bills forwarded from an office; (the "Out Business," as it is called) and the other that of way-bills received, (or, the "In Business"). As these accounts are to be rendered monthly, the following rules will very generally apply.

The first of these settlements, that of the "Out Business," will be known and always referred to as the "Abstract;" and the second, or "In Business," as the "Statement."

THE ABSTRACT.

142. Immediately after the close of a month—that is, on the first day of the succeeding month—an Abstract must be made out, upon the blanks furnished for that purpose, with the date, number, and destination of each way-bill sent during the month just ended, and the total amounts, if any, of the several charges columns of the same, each under its proper heading.

Time of making abstract.

Form.

143. All bills sent to any one office will be reported in consecutive order on the Abstract, (and also on the Statement) as to numbers and dates, and in the following rotation: 1. All bills to San Francisco; 2. All bills to Sacramento; 3. All bills to Marysville; 4. All bills to Stockton; after these all other offices will follow in the order in which they appear on the printed list of offices of Aug. 1, 1868, arranging them consecutively.

Classification of way-bills.

144. When all bills have been thus recorded on the Abstract, the several columns must be correctly footed, and the difference between the "Prepaid," or cash received column, and the "Advanced Charges," or cash disbursed column, will determine the amount of credit due from, or indebtedness to, the General Office at San Francisco.

Balance of Indebtedness.

145. If the result be in favor of the latter, the agent will at once remit to the Cashier of Interior Express at San Francisco, along with his Abstract, the whole amount due thereon.

Balance due General Office to accompany abstract.

146. If the result be found in favor of the agent, he will hold such credit over until the settlement of his "In Business," or "Statement," when he will reimburse himself by reporting the same in part payment of any balance which he may find himself owing on the latter.

Balance due agent to be carried to statement.

Payment of balance.   147. Agents will note at foot of the Abstract what is sent in payment.

Messengers' abstracts.   148. Messengers' Abstracts are to be returned from office settling them, same as its own, except that the name of messenger must be used instead of office.

Numbering abstracts.   149. Abstracts will be numbered 1, 2, 3, etc., in consecutive order, beginning with the first month of each year ; but all the sheets of any one abstract will have the same number.

Reporting all way-bills.   150. Every way-bill made at and sent from an office, must be reported on the Abstract from that office, without regard to whether it contain any charges or not.

Abstract envelopes and labels.   151. Official envelopes in which to inclose Abstracts, and labels for packages, when funds are sent to pay the amount due on an Abstract, will be furnished each office, and are to be used for that purpose only. Remittances for Abstracts and Statements must be made separately.

See form of an Abstract, page 37.

THE STATEMENT.

Statements to be made from way-bills.   152. The Statement, being a report of the "In Business" of an office, consists of an account, classified and arranged as explained in instructions relating to the Abstract, of the way-bills received at an office. Thus the Statement, *which must, in all cases, be made directly from the way-bills*, and upon the book* and blanks furnished for that purpose, gives the amount that each way-bill received calls for.

Under and over charges.   153. If undercharges or overcharges appear noted on a way-bill, the agent will set the former in the "*add*" column of Statement, and the latter in the *deduct* column.

Determining balance.   154. In the final footing of the Statement, he will

---

*Officers are furnished with books in which to keep copies of Statements. Every error will be corrected by sending the agent a notice of the same, whether in his favor or against him. All bills undergo two examinations.

(*Form of an Abstract.*)

WELLS, FARGO & CO.'S EXPRESS.

Abstract of Bills Nos. 183 to 211, forwarded from BENICIA Office,

From July 1st to July 31st, 1863, inclusive.

RECAPITULATION.

(*Total amount of Bills,* $112.25.)

Prepaid charges... ... .£26 00
Advanced charges.,........................ 14 50
Balance................................. 11 50 Due to San Francisco.

No.	Date.	Where to.	Advanced Charges.		Our Charges.		Prepaid.		To be Collected	
	1863.									
183	July 1	San Francisco........	1	00	2	00			3	00
189	" 7	Do.	1	50	1	50	1	50	1	50
195	" 13	Do.			P. O. R.					
199	" 17	Do.	2	00	Free				2	00
202	" 20	Do.			25	00			25	00
184	" 2	Sacramento			2	50	2	50		
185	" 3	Do.			3	00	1	00	2	00
186	" 4	Do.	1	00	4	00	1	00	4	00
187	" 5	Marysville............		50	4	50	1	00	4	00
188	" 6	Do.			6	00	2	50	3	50
189	" 7	Do.	1	00	5	50	1	75	4	75
195	" 13	Stockton.............			7	75	3	50	4	25
199	" 17	Do.			2	50	1	50	1	00
209	" 24	Angels' Camp.........			3	00	1	50	1	50
199	" 17	Brown's Valley.......			1	50			1	50
185	" 3	Chico			2	00		50	1	50
207	" 22	Downieville...........	2	50	4	00	1	00	5	50
189	" 7	El Dorado...........		75	2	50		50	2	75
205	" 21	Forest Hill,...........	1	00	1	50		50	1	00
186	" 4	Georgetown...........							1	00
211	" 25	Heald-burg...........			1	50		50	1	00
192	" 10	Martinez..............				75				75
200	" 18	Placerville			1	75		75	1	00
211	" 25	San Andreas.....	1	00	1	00			2	00
202	" 20	Virginia City..........	1	50	10	00	3	00	8	50
205	" 21	Do.		75	4	00	1	50	3	25
			$14	50	97	75	$26	00	86	25
					14	50			26	00
					$112	25			$112	25

Coin herewith, $11.50.

(Signed,)

.............................,

Agent.

add to the total of "Collect" column (for the amount of which he is accountable) the sum total of undercharges, and from the aggregate of these two columns, he will deduct the sum total of overcharges, and the result will show the sum of his indebtedness.

Credits in payment of balance. 155. The agent will specify, in liquidation of this indebtedness, the nature and amount of disbursements made by him, under proper authority, during the period of time embraced in this Statement; the balance, if any, due him on Abstract, as above instructed; and, for what still remains due by him on Statement, he will promptly forward along with his Statement, way-bills, **Cash to accompany settlement.** and vouchers, funds to cover the same to the Cashier at San Francisco.

Vouchers. 156. For all purchases made or moneys paid, and for which credit is to be claimed as above, receipts, in duplicate, must be taken on the forms provided—the original to be used as a voucher in settlement of Statement, and to accompany the same, and the duplicate to be retained on file in the office where such disbursements are made.

Unauthorized vouchers. 157. Vouchers for disbursements other than those made with the consent or by direction of the Superintendent or Traveling Agent, can be sent with Statement in payment of amounts due, but are liable to be returned if not approved.

Statements to embrace all bills of the month. 158. Statements are to be made out once a month. As they are to embrace all received bills whose dates are to, and include, the last day of the month, agents will wait long enough for such bills to reach them be- **Promptness enjoined.** fore finishing the Statement; but all delay in rendering the account, beyond one of unavoidable necessity, will be considered as neglect of duty, and may lead to more serious consequences.

Not to include bills of a succeeding month. 159. A Statement shall *not* have any bills entered on it that bear date *after* the last day of the month for which it is rendered.

Numbering statements. 160. A Statement bears *one* number, no matter how many sheets are used in making it out, and every way-bill received must be entered thereon, whether it contains anything to collect or not. *Must include all bills within specified time.*

161. The amounts received for monthly accounts or season contracts are to be added to the Statement, after having been otherwise completed as herein directed. *Receipts on season contracts, etc.*

162. Agents will note at the foot of their Statements what they send to pay, specifying the amount of each voucher, and the amount of cash. *Nature of payments to be specified.*

163. Should it happen (which is not probable) that an agent finds a balance due him on Statement, he may request the Cashier to send him the amount due. *Balance due an agent on statement.*

164. The Statement, the way-bills, the vouchers, and the money (if any) *are all to be put up in one package,* and sent by first Express to "Cashier," etc. Address-labels for such packages are furnished, and must be used. *Statements, etc., to be sent in one package.*

165. The way-bills thus returned must all be folded to the same size, about 4 inches by 7 and thus indorsed : *Folding and packing way-bills.*

No. - —— ——-

——— to ——— —— ———

——— —— 186

They must be arranged in the order in which they are entered on the Statement, *and not rolled up* and otherwise deranged.

166. Statements and way-bills *must* be sent to the head office at San Francisco, if possible, by the 7th of the month succeeding. Both Abstracts and Statements must always be made complete and in good shape, and signed by the Agent. *Statements to be made by 5th of succeeding month.*

See form of Statement, page 40.

(Form of a Statement.)

No. 1. •

WELLS, FARGO & CO.'S EXPRESS.

From BENICIA Office.

Statement of Way-Bills and Proceeds returned to SAN FRANCISCO Office, August 7th, 1868.

Advanced Charges.	Prepaid Charges.	FROM	No.	Date of Way-Bill.	Am't to be collected as pr. Way-Bill.	Add for Under Charges.	Deduct for Ov. Charges.
3 00	2 50	San Francisco	183	July 1	7 00		50
	1 50	Do.	190	" 8	2 75	25	
	50	Do.	197	" 15	3 50		
1 00		Do.	205	" 23	1 50		50
18 00	2 00	Do.	213	" 31	21 00		
	50	Sacramento............	187	" 8	1 50	50	
	1 00	Do.	198	" 16	2 00		
1 50	1 50	Do.	207	" 25	3 00		
50	2 00	Do.	215	" 31	3 00		50
		Marysville.............	190	" 8	1 75	25	
1 00	1 50	Do.	207	" 25	2 00		
50	1 00	Stockton..............	175	" 1	2 50		
	50	Do.	190	" 18	2 00		
		Angels' Camp.........	160	" 10	1 00		
1 25		Downieville........... •	255	" 9	2 00		50
	1 00	Georgetown	94	" 18	1 00		
		Iowa Hill............	75	" 5	2 00		
1 50		Placerville	150	" 4	2 50	50	
	50	San José..............	156	" 1	3 00		
		San Andreas..........	112	" 7	1 75		25
	50	Timbuctoo	70	" 8			
50		Ukiah...............	87	" 5	1 50		
1 50		Virginia City.........	183	" 1	3 50		
	50	Do.	210	" 28	2 50		
	2 00	Yreka................	157	" 11	1 50	50	
$30 25					$75 75	2 00	2 25
					25		2
					$75 50		25

Remitted in payment, this day:
      Coin or Check...............$50 50
      Voucher from Catlin......... 12 00
      "   "   Burke......... 13 00

                            $75 50

(Signed,)

..............................,

                            Agent.

CORRESPONDENCE.

167. All communications addressed to an agent, whether by the Gen. Agent, Superintendent, Cashier, Traveling Agent, or other officer of the Company, or the public, in relation to business, must be promptly answered in writing. *Communications to be answered in writing.*

168. In all questions that do not require instant decision, agents will communicate with the Traveling Agent, or the Superintendent at San Francisco, by letter, using the "Official Business" envelope of the Company, with which they are supplied. Letters, etc., of business, affecting the Division over which he has supervision, must be addressed to the Traveling Agent; those referring to accounts to "Cashier;" those referring to letters, to "Letter Department;" to collections "Collection Department," and those of a general character to the "Superintendent," at San Francisco. *Whom to address.*

169. Agents in writing to the General Office will confine themselves in one letter to one particular subject of business—writing a separate letter for each or any other subject. This practice is necessary in order that the matter may be conveniently referred to its proper department. *Letters to be confined to one subject.*

170. All letters, books, and papers connected with the business, sent to an office, must be carefully preserved, and agents should, when practicable, retain copies or memoranda of all important letters written by them on questions of business. *Correspondence, etc., to be preserved.*

BLANKS.

171. All blanks, stationery, and other articles necessary for the transaction of business, will be furnished upon application to the San Francisco Office. Requisitions should be made at least one month before an office will be out of blanks, on a separate slip of paper, addressed to "Cashier Express department, San Francisco. *Requisitions to be made seasonably.*

F

No alteration of size allowed. 172. Agents are not permitted to change the size of any of the blanks provided, by tearing off portions, or pasting them together.

INSTRUCTIONS TO MESSENGERS.

Way-billing. 1. Messengers will make bills of all goods coming into their hands, on their routes, same as an office, and render abstracts of same to Cashier at San Francisco.

Where to bill to. 2. When packages are received for a place on their route where the Company have no office, they must be billed to the office at the end of the route. That office will look to the messenger for the amount " to be collected."

Self-Reliance. 3. Messengers should see that they receive all packages entered on their bills, and must not rely on the representations of agents or clerks.

Checking. 4. They must check each entry on every bill carried by them, with their initial as a check-mark. If any item recorded is short, it must be so noted on the way-bill.

Blank Books. 5. Blank books are provided in which all way-bills are to be entered, and on which the person receiving the same must receipt. Receipt-books are also provided, in which receipts for all matter delivered *en route* are to be taken. (For manner of identification, etc., see previous instruction.)

Transferring to agents. 6. At the end of their route they must require the agent to receive their goods and treasure, and check for same, thereby relieving themselves of responsibility.

Absence from duty prohibited. 7. No messenger can be allowed to absent himself from duty, by substituting another person to act in his stead, without special permission from the Superintendent, except in case of illness.

Reporting detentions. 8. When a messenger is detained by accident or serious difficulties on his route, he must at once telegraph information of the fact to the point of his destination, and, if deemed necessary, to the point from whence he came.

9. They must be courteous and obliging to all persons with whom they have business, conciliating their good-will, and especially on stage routes, to the passengers. No excuse will be taken from a messenger for insulting or incommoding a stage passenger. Stage passengers.

10. Particular pains must be taken by messengers to deliver letters promptly along their routes. They must each keep a supply of franks constantly on hand, to furnish any person who may want them on the route. Letters and franks.

11. When, upon railroad lines, a separate car, or apartment, is furnished for their exclusive use, messengers will not allow any person to ride therein except by consent of the Traveling Agent or Superintendent. Special cars.

12. When express goods are carried in freight cars, and permission is had to ride in another part of the train, their condition must be examined at every stopping-place. Goods in separate cars.

13. Tariffs will be furnished by each Traveling Agent. In making charges on matter received and billed by messengers, they will charge same as having been sent from the office just passed. Charges.

14. Messengers will make out an abstract, at the end of each month, of the way-bills issued by themselves, and will settle them same as an office. (See paragraphs 142 to 151.) Abstracts.

15. Messengers are required to read and follow the General Instructions to Agents and Employés given in this book, and especially such portions thereof as relate to the General Instructions.

IDENTIFICATION OF UNKNOWN PERSONS.
(See Sec. 17, page 13.)
CARE IN HANDLING GOODS.
(See Secs. 85, 86, etc., page 26.)
RESPONSIBILITY IN DELIVERING TO PROPER PARTIES.
(See Sec. 19, page 14.)
DRINKING INTOXICATING LIQUORS.
(See Sec. 5, page 12.)
MAKING AND NUMBERING WAY-BILLS.
(See Secs. 67 to 77 inc., pages 21 and 24.)
HOW TO MAKE ABSTRACTS.
(See Form, page 37.)

INSTRUCTIONS TO TRAVELING AGENTS.

General duties.

1. Traveling Agents are employed by, and subject to, the orders of the Superintendent at San Francisco, to whom they will look for instructions, and will confer with him in regard to any matter outside of the general detail. They will also keep him fully advised as to their movements and actions.

Visiting offices and examining accounts.

2. It will be the duty of Traveling Agents to visit, as often as practicable, each office in their respective divisions, for the purpose of affording instruction, giving counsel and information, examining accounts and investigating the manner in which the business is conducted.

Office employés.

3. They are expected to see that no more persons are employed at an office, or on any route, than are necessary for the prompt and economical transaction of the business, and that no person is continued in the employ whose private acts or character tend to injure the good name of the Company.

Authority over employés.

4. In all cases of incapacity or inattention to business on the part of agents and employés, the Traveling Agent will confer, at once, with the Superintendent at San Francisco, and be governed by his instructions, except in cases of emergency, when the Traveling Agent will summarily discharge such person, and make temporary arrangements for the safe transaction of business at such point, until the case is referred to, and decided upon by, the Superintendent.

Handling freight.

5. They will be particular to see that freight is handled carefully by the respective agents, messengers, and drivers in their division, and where damage occurs from carelessness, either collect the amount of damage from the employé causing said damage, or discharge him.

Office fixtures.

6. In authorizing purchases of fixtures, or personal property, they will make themselves acquainted with the necessity of the same before granting the authority, and

all vouchers for such expenses must be approved by them in writing.

7. All contracts with transportation lines, with bankers, or others, for season contracts ; all offices opened or discontinued, agents, messengers, or men employed or discharged, and, in fact, a general report of their transactions, must be made to the Superintendent at San Francisco, promptly. *Contracts and changes.*

8. In opening new, or closing old offices, notice must be given to *all offices and messengers* under *their supervision*, and to San Francisco Office, stating name and place, and tariff to same, or if for closing an office, state to *what point* such matter must be *billed thereafter*. *Information relating to change of Offices.*

9. At points where the Company have horses and wagons, Traveling Agents will make it their particular business to see that such property is kept in good condition, and as well and economically taken care of as possible. *Care of property.*

GENERAL TARIFF, WELLS, FARGO & CO'S EXPRESS.

*To or from Offices designated thus, Agents will add one half per cent. for INSURANCE on Marine Risks. The above Tariff will not interfere with any existing Special or Season Contracts. On Packages or Treasure for points on Overland Routes to Oregon or Los Angeles, charge 10 cents per lb. per 100 miles, and ½ per cent. on Treasure per 100 miles.

NOTE.—The rates from any office to San Francisco or Sacramento added to the rate from these points to destination will give the rate to be charged.

OFFICES.	TO AND FROM SAN FRANCISCO.							TO AND FROM SACRAMENTO.						
	FREIGHT. Per lb.			TREASURE. Per cent.				FREIGHT. Per lb.			TREASURE. Per cent.			
	Under 50 lbs.	Over 50 lbs.	Over 100 lbs.	Over $100.	Over $300.	Over $500.	Over $1000.	Under 50 lbs.	Over 50 lbs.	Over 100 lbs.	Over $100.	Over $300.	Over $500.	Over $1000.
Angel's Camp,	10	9	8	¾	½	½	⅜	10	9	8	¾	½	½	⅜
Auburn,	4	3	2	½	⅜	¼	⅛	4	3	2	½	⅜	¼	⅛
Albion,	10	9	8	1	⅞	¾	¾	10	10	9	1	1	⅞	¾
Amador City,	9	8	8	¾	½	⅜	¼	9	8	7	½	⅜	¼	¼
*Arcata, H. B.	4	4	3	1	⅞	¾	⅝	5	4	3	1	1	⅞	¾
*Anaheim,	5	4	4	1	1	¾	½	5	4	4	1	1	1	¾
Aurora, Nev.	22	21	20	2	1¾	1½	1½	22	21	20	2	1¾	1½	1½
Austin, Nev.	22	21	20	2	2	1¾	1½	22	21	20	2	2	1¾	1½

*Albany, Or.	10	9	8	2	1½	1¼	1	10	9	8	2	1½	1¼	1
*Astoria, Or.	4	3	2	1¼	¾	¾	½	5	4	3	1¼	¾	¾	⅝
Antioch,	2	2	1	½	⅜	¼	⅛	2	2	1	½	⅜	¼	⅛
Benicia,	2	2	1	½	⅜	¼	⅛	2	2	1	½	⅜	¼	⅛
Bear Valley,	12	11	10	1	⅞	¾	⅝	13	13	12	1	1	⅞	¾
Big Oak Flat,	12	11	10	1	¾	¾	⅝	14	13	12	1	1	¾	¾
Bloomfield,	5	4	3	¾	½	⅜	¼	6	5	4	1	¾	⅝	⅜
Bodega,	5	4	3	¾	½	⅜	¼	6	5	4	1	¾	⅝	⅜
Boise City, Idaho,	40	38	35	3½	3¼	3	2½	40	38	35	3½	3¼	3	2½
*Baker City, Or.	20	18	15	3	2½	2¼	2	20	18	15	3	2½	2¼	2
Brown's Valley,	8	7	6	¾	¾	½	¼	7	7	6	¾	¾	½	¼
Belmont, Nev.	32	31	30	2½	2¼	2	2	32	31	30	2½	2¼	2	2
Belmont,	2	2	1	½	¼	⅛	⅛	3	2	2	½	⅜	⅜	¼
*Crescent City,	3	3	2	1	⅞	¾	⅝	4	3	3	1	1	⅞	¾
Calistoga,	5	4	3	¾	½	⅜	¼	5	5	4	1	¾	⅜	⅜
Campo Seco,	8	7	6	¾	½	⅜	¼	10	8	8	¾	½	⅜	¼

GENERAL TARIFF—Continued.

OFFICES.	TO AND FROM SAN FRANCISCO. FREIGHT. Per lb. Under 50 lbs.	Over 50 lbs.	Over 100 lbs.	TREASURE. Per cent. Over $100.	Over $300.	Over $500.	Over $1000.	TO AND FROM SACRAMENTO. FREIGHT. Per lb. Under 50 lbs.	Over 50 lbs.	Over 100 lbs.	TREASURE. Per cent. Over $100.	Over $300.	Over $500.	Over $1000.
Coloma,	7	6	5	3/4	1/2	3/8	1/4	7	6	5	3/4	1/2	3/8	1/4
Columbia,	10	9	9	3/4	1/2	1/2	3/8	12	11	10	3/4	1/2	1/2	3/8
Chinese,	9	8	8	3/4	5/8	1/2	3/8	12	11	10	3/4	1/2	1/2	3/8
Cloverdale,	6	5	4	3/4	1/2	3/8	1/4	7	6	5	1	3/4	1/2	3/8
Camanche,	10	9	8	3/4	1/2	3/8	1/4	12	11	10	3/4	5/8	1/2	1/2
Coulterville,	15	14	13	1	7/8	3/4	5/8	17	16	15	1	3/4	3/4	3/4
Carson City, Nev.	8	7	6	1	3/4	5/8	1/2	8	7	6	1	3/4	5/8	1/2
Cacheville,	5	4	4	3/4	5/8	1/2	1/4	5	4	4	3/4	1/2	3/8	1/4
Callahan's Ranch,	28	27	25	2	1 3/4	1 3/8	1 1/4	28	27	25	2	1 3/4	1 3/8	1/4
Copperopolis,	10	9	8	3/4	1/2	3/8	1/4	12	11	10	1	3/4	1/2	3/8
*Corvallis, Or.	10	8	5	2	1 3/4	1 1/2	1	10	8	5	2	1 3/4	1 1/2	1

Chico,

G Centreville, Idaho,

Cañonville, Or.

Colfax,

Crystal Peak, Nev.

Camptonville,

Cisco,

Columbus House,

Clipper Mills,

Collinsville,

Castroville,

Coburn's,

Colusa,

Drytown,

Diamond Springs,

Duncan's Mill,

GENERAL TARIFF—Continued.

OFFICES.	TO AND FROM SAN FRANCISCO. FREIGHT. Per lb. Under 50 lbs.	Over 50 lbs.	Over 100 lbs.	TREASURE. Per cent. Over $100.	Over $300.	Over $500.	Over $1000.	TO AND FROM SACRAMENTO. FREIGHT. Per lb. Under 50 lbs.	Over 50 lbs.	Over 100 lbs.	TREASURE. Per cent. Over $100.	Over $300.	Over $500.	Over $1000.
Dutch Flat,	5	4	3	$\frac{1}{2}$	$\frac{3}{8}$	$\frac{1}{4}$	$\frac{1}{8}$	4	3	2	$\frac{1}{2}$	$\frac{3}{8}$	$\frac{1}{4}$	$\frac{1}{8}$
Dayton, Nev.	9	8	7	1	1	$\frac{3}{4}$	$\frac{5}{8}$	9	8	7	1	1	$\frac{3}{4}$	$\frac{5}{8}$
*Dalles, Or.	8	7	6	1	1	$\frac{3}{4}$	$\frac{1}{2}$	9	8	7	1	1	$\frac{3}{4}$	$\frac{5}{8}$
Downieville,	12	11	10	1	$\frac{7}{8}$	$\frac{3}{4}$	$\frac{5}{8}$	12	11	10	1	$\frac{7}{8}$	$\frac{3}{4}$	$\frac{5}{8}$
Dunn Glen, Nev.	27	26	25	2	$1\frac{3}{4}$	$1\frac{5}{8}$	$1\frac{1}{2}$	27	26	25	2	$1\frac{3}{4}$	$1\frac{5}{8}$	$1\frac{1}{2}$
El Dorado,	5	4	4	$\frac{3}{4}$	$\frac{1}{2}$	$\frac{1}{4}$	$\frac{1}{8}$	5	4	3	$\frac{3}{4}$	$\frac{1}{2}$	$\frac{1}{4}$	$\frac{1}{8}$
*Eureka, H. B.	3	3	2	1	$\frac{7}{8}$	$\frac{3}{4}$	$\frac{5}{8}$	4	3	3	1	1	$\frac{7}{8}$	$\frac{3}{4}$
*Eugene City, Or.	22	21	20	$1\frac{1}{2}$	$1\frac{1}{4}$	$\frac{7}{8}$	$\frac{3}{4}$	22	21	20	$1\frac{1}{2}$	$1\frac{1}{4}$	1	1
Empire Ranch,	8	7	6	$\frac{3}{4}$	$\frac{1}{2}$	$\frac{3}{8}$	$\frac{1}{4}$	7	6	5	$\frac{3}{4}$	$\frac{1}{2}$	$\frac{1}{4}$	$\frac{1}{4}$
Emigrant Gap,	4	3	2	$\frac{1}{2}$	$\frac{3}{8}$	$\frac{1}{4}$	$\frac{1}{8}$	3	3	2	$\frac{1}{2}$	$\frac{3}{8}$	$\frac{1}{4}$	$\frac{1}{8}$
Folsom,	3	3	2	$\frac{3}{4}$	$\frac{1}{2}$	$\frac{1}{4}$	$\frac{1}{8}$	3	2	1	$\frac{3}{4}$	$\frac{1}{2}$	$\frac{1}{4}$	$\frac{1}{8}$

Fiddletown,	10	9	8	7	1	$\frac{3}{4}$	$\frac{1}{2}$	$\frac{3}{8}$	$\frac{1}{4}$	9	8	7	$\frac{3}{4}$	$\frac{1}{2}$	$\frac{3}{8}$	$\frac{1}{4}$
Forest Hill,	8	7	6	5	$\frac{3}{4}$	$\frac{3}{4}$	$\frac{1}{2}$	$\frac{3}{8}$	$\frac{1}{4}$	8	7	6	$\frac{3}{4}$	$\frac{1}{2}$	$\frac{3}{8}$	$\frac{1}{4}$
Franktown, Nev.	8	7	6	5	1	1	$\frac{3}{4}$	$\frac{5}{8}$	$\frac{1}{2}$	8	7	6	1	$\frac{3}{4}$	$\frac{5}{8}$	$\frac{1}{2}$
French Corral,	9	8	7	6	$\frac{3}{4}$	$\frac{3}{4}$	$\frac{1}{2}$	$\frac{3}{8}$	$\frac{1}{4}$	9	8	7	$\frac{3}{4}$	$\frac{1}{2}$	$\frac{3}{8}$	$\frac{1}{4}$
Forest City,	12	11	10	10	1	1	$\frac{3}{4}$	$\frac{1}{2}$	$\frac{3}{8}$	12	11	10	1	$\frac{3}{4}$	$\frac{1}{2}$	$\frac{3}{8}$
Forbestown,	9	8	7	7	1	$\frac{3}{4}$	$\frac{3}{4}$	$\frac{1}{2}$	$\frac{1}{2}$	9	8	7	$\frac{3}{4}$	$\frac{1}{2}$	$\frac{1}{2}$	$\frac{3}{8}$
Fort Jones,	28	27	25	25	2	1$\frac{1}{2}$	1$\frac{1}{4}$	1$\frac{1}{8}$	1$\frac{1}{4}$	27	26	25	2	1$\frac{1}{2}$	1$\frac{1}{8}$	1$\frac{1}{4}$
Grass Valley,	7	6	5	5	$\frac{3}{4}$	$\frac{1}{2}$	$\frac{3}{8}$	$\frac{1}{4}$	7	6	5	$\frac{3}{4}$	$\frac{1}{2}$	$\frac{3}{8}$	$\frac{1}{4}$	
Georgetown,	8	7	6	5	$\frac{3}{4}$	$\frac{1}{2}$	$\frac{3}{8}$	$\frac{1}{4}$	8	7	6	$\frac{3}{4}$	$\frac{1}{2}$	$\frac{3}{8}$	$\frac{1}{4}$	
Greenwood,	8	7	6	5	$\frac{3}{4}$	$\frac{1}{2}$	$\frac{3}{8}$	$\frac{1}{4}$	8	7	6	$\frac{3}{4}$	$\frac{1}{2}$	$\frac{5}{8}$	$\frac{1}{2}$	
Gold Hill, Nev.	8	7	6	5	1	$\frac{3}{4}$	$\frac{3}{4}$	$\frac{1}{2}$	$\frac{3}{8}$	8	7	6	1	$\frac{3}{4}$	$\frac{1}{2}$	$\frac{3}{8}$
Gilroy,	5	4	3	4	$\frac{3}{4}$	$\frac{3}{4}$	$\frac{5}{8}$	$\frac{1}{2}$	5	5	4	$\frac{1}{2}$	$\frac{1}{2}$	$\frac{1}{2}$	$\frac{1}{2}$	
Geyserville,	6	5	4	6	1	$\frac{3}{4}$	$\frac{1}{2}$	$\frac{3}{8}$	6	6	5	$\frac{3}{4}$	$\frac{5}{8}$	$\frac{1}{2}$	$\frac{3}{8}$	
Genoa, Nev.	10	9	8	8	1$\frac{3}{4}$	1	1	1$\frac{7}{8}$	$\frac{3}{4}$	10	9	8	1	1	$\frac{7}{8}$	$\frac{3}{4}$
*Guaymas, Mex.	5	4	3	2	1	1	1$\frac{1}{2}$	1$\frac{1}{4}$	1	6	5	4	1	1$\frac{1}{2}$	1$\frac{1}{4}$	1
Gold Run,	4	3	2	2	2	1$\frac{1}{2}$	$\frac{3}{8}$	$\frac{1}{4}$	$\frac{1}{8}$	4	3	2	$\frac{1}{2}$	$\frac{3}{8}$	$\frac{1}{4}$	$\frac{1}{8}$

GENERAL TARIFF—Continued.

OFFICES.	To and from San Francisco. Freight. Per lb. Under 50 lbs.	Over 50 lbs.	Over 100 lbs.	Treasure. Per cent. Over $100.	Over $300.	Over $500.	Over $1000.	To and from Sacramento. Freight. Per lb. Under 50 lbs.	Over 50 lbs.	Over 100 lbs.	Treasure. Per cent. Over $100.	Over $300.	Over $500.	Over $1000.
Gibsonville,	15	14	13	1	1	⅞	¾	14	13	12	1	1	¾	⅝
Goodyear's Bar,	11	10	9	1	¾	⅝	½	10	9	8	¾	⅝	½	⅜
Hamilton, Nev.	30	29	28	3	3	2¾	2½	30	29	28	3	3	2¾	2½
*Honolulu, S. I.	6	5	4	2	2	1½	1½	6	5	4	2½	2¼	2	2
Hornitos,	11	10	9	1	¾	¾	⅝	12	12	11	1	¾	¾	⅝
Healdsburg,	6	5	4	¾	½	⅜	¼	6	5	5	1	¾	½	⅜
Huffaker's, Nev.	6	5	4	1	¾	½	½	6	5	4	1	¾	½	½
Howland's Flat,	15	14	13	1	1	⅞	¾	14	13	12	1	1	¾	⅝
Havilah,	25	23	22	2	1¾	1½	1¼	25	23	22	2	1¾	1½	1½
Ione Valley,	8	7	7	¾	½	⅜	⅜	8	7	6	¾	½	⅜	¼
Iowa Hill,	8	7	7	¾	⅝	½	⅜	8	7	6	¾	⅝	½	⅜

Idaho City, Idaho,	45	43	40	3½	3¼	3	2¾	45	43	40	3½	3¼	3	2¾
Jackson,	10	9	8	¾	½	⅜	¼	.8	7	7	¾	½	⅜	¼
Jamestown,	10	9	8	¾	⅝	½	⅜	12	11	11	¾	⅝	½	½
Jenny Lind,	8	7	7	¾	½	⅜	⅜	12	11	10	¾	⅝	½	⅜
Jacksonville, Or.	40	37	35	2½	2¼	2	1¾	40	37	35	2½	2	2	1¾
Kingston,	15	14	13	1	1	⅞	¾	15	15	14	1½	1¼	⅞	¾
Kernville,	25	22	20	2	1¾	1½	1½	25	22	20	2	2	1¾	1½
Knight's Ferry,	8	7	6	¾	½	⅜	¼	10	9	8	¾	⅝	½	⅜
Knight's Landing,	5	4	3	¾	½	⅜	¼	5	4	3	¾	½	⅜	¼
Knoxville,	6	5	4	¾	½	⅜	¼	6	5	4	¾	½	⅜	¼
Lawrence's,	2	1	1	½	⅜	¼	⅛	3	2	2	¾	⅝	½	¼
*Los Angeles,	5	4	3	1	¾	⅝	½	5	4	4	1	¾	⅝	½
Lakeport,	8	7	7	1	¾	⅝	½	9	8	8	1	1	¾	⅝
Lower Lake,	8	7	7	1	¾	¾	½	8	8	7	1	1	¾	¾
Lancha Plana,	8	7	6	¾	½	⅜	¼	12	11	10	¾	½	⅜	¼
Lincoln,	3	3	2	¾	⅜	¼	⅛	3	2	2	½	⅜	¼	⅛

GENERAL TARIFF—Continued.

OFFICES.	TO AND FROM SAN FRANCISCO. FREIGHT. Per lb. Under 50 lbs.	Over 50 lbs.	Over 100 lbs.	TREASURE. Per cent. Over $100.	Over $300.	Over $500.	Over $1000.	TO AND FROM SACRAMENTO. FREIGHT. Per lb. Under 50 lbs.	Over 50 lbs.	Over 100 lbs.	TREASURE. Per cent. Over $100.	Over $300.	Over $500.	Over $1000.
*Lewiston, Idaho,	20	18	15	2	1¾	1½	1¼	20	18	15	2	1¾	1½	1½
*La Paz, Mex.	5	4	3	2	1½	1¼	1	5	4	3	2	1½	1¼	1
Latrobe,	3	2	2	¾	½	¼	⅛	3	2	2	¾	½	¼	⅛
*La Grande, Or.	25	22	20	2½	2¼	2	2	25	22	20	2½	2¼	2	2
Laporte,	14	13	12	1	1	¾	⅝	14	13	12	1	¾	⅝	½
Linden,	5	4	3	½	⅜	¼	¼	7	6	5	¾	½	⅜	⅜
Longville,	15	14	12	1½	1¼	1	¾	14	13	12	1½	1¼	1	¾
Marysville,	5	4	3	½	⅜	¼	⅛	5	4	3	½	⅜	¼	⅛
Mariposa,	12	11	10	1	1	¾	⅝	15	13	12	1	1	¾	¾
Michigan Bar,	7	7	6	¾	½	⅜	¼	6	6	5	¾	½	⅜	¼
Michigan Bluff,	8	7	6	¾	⅝	⅜	¼	8	7	6	¾	⅝	⅜	¼

Monticello,	5	4	4	$\frac{3}{4}$	$\frac{1}{2}$	$\frac{3}{8}$	$\frac{1}{4}$	5	4	4	$\frac{3}{4}$	$\frac{1}{2}$	$\frac{3}{8}$
Moquelumne Hill,	10	9	8	$\frac{3}{4}$	$\frac{1}{2}$	$\frac{3}{8}$	$\frac{1}{4}$	8	8	7	$\frac{3}{4}$	$\frac{1}{2}$	$\frac{3}{8}$
Murphy's Camp,	10	9	9	$\frac{3}{4}$	$\frac{5}{8}$	$\frac{1}{2}$	$\frac{5}{8}$	10	10	9	$\frac{5}{8}$	$\frac{1}{2}$	$\frac{3}{8}$
Mendocino City,	12	11	10	1	1	1	1	13	12	11	1	1	$\frac{3}{4}$
Martinez,	3	2	1	$\frac{1}{2}$	$\frac{3}{8}$	$\frac{1}{4}$	$\frac{1}{8}$	3	2	1	$\frac{1}{2}$	$\frac{3}{8}$	$\frac{1}{8}$
Menlo Park,	2	1	1	$\frac{1}{2}$	$\frac{3}{8}$	$\frac{1}{4}$	$\frac{1}{8}$	3	2	1	$\frac{3}{4}$	$\frac{1}{2}$	$\frac{1}{4}$
Monterey,	8	7	7	1	$\frac{3}{4}$	$\frac{5}{8}$	$\frac{1}{2}$	9	8	8	1	$\frac{3}{4}$	$\frac{5}{8}$
Millerton,	16	15	15	$1\frac{1}{4}$	1	$\frac{7}{8}$	$\frac{7}{8}$	17	16	16	$1\frac{1}{4}$	1	$\frac{7}{8}$
Markleeville,	17	16	15	2	2	$1\frac{3}{4}$	$1\frac{1}{2}$	17	16	15	2	2	$1\frac{1}{2}$
*Mazatlan, Mex.	5	4	3	$1\frac{1}{2}$	$1\frac{1}{4}$	$1\frac{1}{4}$	1	5	4	4	$1\frac{1}{2}$	$1\frac{1}{4}$	1
Mayfield,	2	1	1	$\frac{1}{2}$	$\frac{3}{8}$	$\frac{1}{4}$	$\frac{1}{8}$	3	2	2	$\frac{3}{4}$	$\frac{1}{2}$	$\frac{1}{4}$
Napa City,	2	1	1	$\frac{1}{2}$	$\frac{3}{8}$	$\frac{1}{4}$	$\frac{1}{8}$	3	2	2	$\frac{3}{4}$	$\frac{1}{2}$	$\frac{1}{4}$
Nevada,	7	6	5	$\frac{3}{4}$	$\frac{1}{2}$	$\frac{3}{8}$	$\frac{1}{4}$	7	6	5	$\frac{3}{4}$	$\frac{1}{2}$	$\frac{1}{4}$
Newcastle,	4	3	2	$\frac{1}{2}$	$\frac{3}{8}$	$\frac{1}{4}$	$\frac{1}{8}$	3	2	2	$\frac{1}{2}$	$\frac{3}{8}$	$\frac{1}{8}$
North San Juan,	9	8	7	1	$\frac{3}{8}$	$\frac{1}{2}$	$\frac{3}{8}$	9	8	7	1	$\frac{3}{4}$	$\frac{3}{8}$
Oroville,	6	5	4	$\frac{1}{2}$	$\frac{1}{2}$	$\frac{1}{4}$	$\frac{1}{4}$	6	5	4	$\frac{1}{2}$	$\frac{3}{8}$	$\frac{1}{4}$

GENERAL TARIFF—Continued.

OFFICES.	TO AND FROM SAN FRANCISCO.							TO AND FROM SACRAMENTO.						
	FREIGHT. Per lb.			TREASURE. Per cent.				FREIGHT. Per lb.			TREASURE. Per cent.			
	Under 50 lbs.	Over 50 lbs.	Over 100 lbs.	Over $100.	Over $300.	Over $500.	Over $1000.	Under 50 lbs.	Over 50 lbs.	Over 100 lbs.	Over $100.	Over $300.	Over $500.	Over $1000.
*Olympia, W. T.	5	4	4	1	1	$\frac{3}{4}$	$\frac{5}{8}$	6	5	4	1	1	1	$\frac{3}{4}$
Ophir,	8	7	6	1	$\frac{3}{4}$	$\frac{5}{8}$	$\frac{1}{2}$	8	7	6	1	$\frac{3}{4}$	$\frac{5}{8}$	$\frac{1}{2}$
*Oakland, Or.	27	26	25	2$\frac{1}{4}$	2$\frac{1}{4}$	1$\frac{3}{4}$	1$\frac{1}{2}$	27	26	25	2$\frac{1}{4}$	2$\frac{1}{4}$	1$\frac{3}{4}$	1$\frac{1}{4}$
*Oregon City, Or.	5	4	3	1	1	$\frac{3}{4}$	$\frac{5}{8}$	6	5	4	1	1	$\frac{3}{4}$	$\frac{5}{8}$
Oreana, Nev.	22	21	20	2	1$\frac{3}{4}$	1$\frac{1}{2}$	1$\frac{1}{4}$	22	21	20	2	1$\frac{3}{4}$	1$\frac{1}{2}$	1$\frac{1}{4}$
*Portland, Or.	3	2	2	1	1	$\frac{3}{4}$	$\frac{5}{8}$	4	3	2	1	1$\frac{3}{4}$	1$\frac{1}{2}$	1$\frac{1}{4}$
Pescadero,	4	3	2	$\frac{3}{4}$	$\frac{3}{4}$	$\frac{5}{8}$	$\frac{1}{2}$	5	4	3	$\frac{3}{4}$	$\frac{1}{2}$	$\frac{3}{8}$	$\frac{1}{4}$
Petaluma,	2	1$\frac{1}{2}$	1	1$\frac{1}{2}$	1$\frac{1}{2}$	$\frac{3}{8}$	$\frac{3}{8}$	3	2	2	$\frac{3}{4}$	$\frac{1}{2}$	$\frac{3}{8}$	$\frac{1}{4}$
Placerville,	5	4	4	$\frac{3}{4}$	$\frac{3}{4}$	$\frac{5}{8}$	$\frac{1}{2}$	5	4	3	$\frac{3}{4}$	$\frac{1}{2}$	$\frac{1}{4}$	$\frac{1}{8}$
Pacheco,	3	3	2	1$\frac{1}{2}$	1$\frac{1}{2}$	$\frac{3}{4}$	$\frac{3}{8}$	4	3	3	$\frac{3}{4}$	$\frac{1}{2}$	$\frac{1}{4}$	$\frac{1}{4}$
Placerville, Idaho,	50	47	45	4	3$\frac{1}{2}$	3$\frac{1}{2}$	3	50	47	45	4	3$\frac{1}{2}$	3$\frac{1}{2}$	3

Pioneer City, Idaho,	50	47	45	4	3½	3¼	3	50	47	45	4	3½	3¼	3
Pine Grove, Nev.	12	11	10	1½	1¼	1	1	12	11	10	1½	1¼	1	1
Paradise City,	5	4	4	¾	½	⅜	¼	7	6	5	1	¾	½	½
Quincy,	15	14	13	1¼	1¼	1	¾	15	14	13	1¼	1¼	1	¾
Red Bluffs,	15	14	14	1	¾	½	⅜	15	14	14	1	¾	½	⅜
Rough & Ready,	8	7	6	¾	½	⅜	¼	8	7	6	¾	½	⅜	¼
Redwood City,	2	1	1	½	⅜	¼	⅛	3	2	2	¾	½	⅜	¼
Ruby Valley, Nev.	35	32	30	2½	2½	2¼	2	35	32	30	2½	2½	2¼	2
*Roseburg, Or.	27	26	25	2½	2½	2¼	2	27	26	25	2½	2½	2¼	2
Round Valley,	18	16	15	1½	1¼	1	¾	18	16	15	1½	1¼	1	¾
Ruby City, Idaho,	35	33	30	3½	3¼	3	2½	35	33	30	3½	3¼	3	2½
Reno, Nev.	5	5	4	¾	½	½	⅜	5	5	4	¾	½	½	⅜
Rocklin,	3	2	2	½	⅜	¼	⅛	2	1	1	½	⅜	¼	⅛
Rio Vista,	2	2	1	½	⅜	¼	⅛	2	2	1	½	⅜	¼	⅛
Shasta,	20	19	18	1	¾	⅝	½	20	19	18	1	¾	⅝	½
San Andres,	10	9	8	¾	¾	½	⅜	12	11	10	1	¾	½	⅜

GENERAL TARIFF—Continued.

OFFICES.	TO AND FROM SAN FRANCISCO.							TO AND FROM SACRAMENTO.						
	FREIGHT. Per lb.			TREASURE. Per cent.				FREIGHT. Per lb.			TREASURE. Per cent.			
	Under 50 lbs.	Over 50 lbs.	Over 100 lbs.	Over $100.	Over $300.	Over $500.	Over $1000.	Under 50 lbs.	Over 50 lbs.	Over 100 lbs.	Over $100.	Over $300.	Over $500.	Over $1000.
San José,	2	1½	1	1½	3⁄8	1⁄4	1⁄4	3	2	2	1	3⁄4	1⁄2	1⁄4
Santa Clara,	2	1½	1	1½	3⁄8	1⁄4	1⁄4	3	2	2	1	3⁄4	1⁄2	1⁄4
Sebastopol,	5	4	3	3⁄4	1⁄2	3⁄8	3⁄8	5	4	4	1	3⁄4	1⁄2	3⁄8
St. Helena,	6	5½	5	3⁄4	3⁄4	1⁄2	3⁄8	7	6	6	1	3⁄4	1⁄2	3⁄8
Sonoma,	4	3	3	3⁄4	5⁄8	1⁄2	3⁄8	5	4	4	1	3⁄4	1⁄2	3⁄8
Sutter Creek,	10	9	8	3⁄4	1⁄2	1⁄4	1⁄4	10	9	8	1½	3⁄4	1⁄4	1⁄4
Sacramento,	2	1½	1	1⁄2	3⁄8	1⁄4	1⁄8							
Stockton,	2	1½	1	1⁄2	3⁄8	1⁄4	1⁄8	4	3	3	3⁄4	1⁄2	3⁄8	1⁄4
Sonora,	10	9	9	1	3⁄4	1⁄2	3⁄8	12	12	11	1	3⁄4	1⁄2	1⁄2
Suisun,	3	2	2	1⁄2	1⁄4	1⁄4	1⁄8	3	2	2	3⁄4	1⁄2	3⁄8	1⁄4
San Juan, South,	5	5	4	3⁄4	1⁄2	1⁄2	1⁄4	6	5	5	1	3⁄4	3⁄8	3⁄8

Santa Cruz,	6	5	5	½	½	⅜	¼	7	6	6	¾	½	½	⅜
*Santa Barbara,	3	3	2	1	1	¾	½	5	4	3	1	1	¾	⅝
*San Bernardino,	10	9	8	2	1½	1¼	1	10	9	8	2	1½	1½	1¼
San Luis Obispo,	16	15	14	1½	1¼	1¼	1	16	15	15	1½	1¼	1¼	1
San Rafael,	2	1	1	½	⅜	¼	⅛	3	2	2	¾	½	⅜	¼
San Quentin,	2	1	1	½	⅜	¼	⅛	3	2	2	¾	½	⅜	¼
Santa Rosa,	4	3½	3	½	½	⅜	¼	5	4	4	¾	½	½	⅜
Silver City, Nev.	8	7	7	1	1	¾	⅝	8	7	7	1	1	¾	½
Snellings,	10	9	8	1	1	¾	⅝	12	11	10	1	1	¾	⅝
San Mateo,	2	1	1	½	⅜	¼	⅛	3	2	2	¾	½	⅜	¼
*Salem, Or.	12	11	10	1	1	¾	¾	12	11	10	1	1	¾	¾
Salt Lake City, Utah,	45	44	43	3	2¾	2¾	2½	45	44	43	3	2¾	2½	2½
Shingle Springs,	4	3	3	½	⅜	¼	⅛	4	3	2	½	⅜	¼	⅛
Silver Mountain,	17	16	15	2	2	1¾	1½	17	16	15	2	2	1¾	1½
Smartsville,	9	8	7	¾	½	⅜	¼	9	8	7	¾	½	⅜	¼
Susanville,	18	16	15	1½	1¼	1	1	17	16	15	1½	1¼	1	1

GENERAL TARIFF—Continued.

OFFICES.	TO AND FROM SAN FRANCISCO.							TO AND FROM SACRAMENTO.						
	FREIGHT. Per lb.			TREASURE. Per cent.				FREIGHT. Per lb.			TREASURE. Per cent.			
	Under 50 lbs.	Over 50 lbs.	Over 100 lbs.	Over $100.	Over $300.	Over $500.	Over $1000.	Under 50 lbs.	Over 50 lbs.	Over 100 lbs.	Over $100.	Over $300.	Over $500.	Over $1000.
St. Louis,	15	14	13	1	1	$\frac{7}{8}$	$\frac{3}{4}$	15	13	12	1	1	$\frac{7}{8}$	$\frac{3}{4}$
Spanish Ranch,	15	13	12	1	1	$\frac{7}{8}$	$\frac{3}{4}$	15	13	12	1	1	$\frac{7}{8}$	$\frac{3}{4}$
Spanish Town,	4	3	3	$1\frac{1}{2}$	$1\frac{1}{4}$	$\frac{3}{8}$	$\frac{1}{4}$	5	4	4	$\frac{3}{4}$	$1\frac{1}{2}$	$\frac{3}{8}$	$\frac{3}{8}$
*San Buenaventura,	20	19	18	$1\frac{1}{2}$	$1\frac{1}{2}$	$1\frac{1}{4}$	1	20	19	18	$1\frac{1}{2}$	$1\frac{1}{2}$	$1\frac{1}{4}$	1
*San Diego,	5	4	3	$1\frac{1}{2}$	$1\frac{1}{4}$	$\frac{3}{4}$	$\frac{5}{8}$	5	4	4	$1\frac{1}{2}$	$1\frac{1}{4}$	$\frac{3}{4}$	$\frac{3}{4}$
Silveyville,	4	3	3	$\frac{3}{4}$	$1\frac{1}{2}$	$\frac{3}{8}$	$\frac{1}{4}$	5	4	4	$1\frac{1}{2}$	$1\frac{1}{2}$	$\frac{3}{4}$	$\frac{3}{4}$
Sweetland,	9	8	7	$1\frac{1}{2}$	$\frac{3}{4}$	$\frac{1}{2}$	$\frac{3}{8}$	10	9	8	$\frac{3}{4}$	$\frac{1}{2}$	$\frac{3}{8}$	$\frac{1}{4}$
Searsville,	3	2	2	$1\frac{1}{2}$	$\frac{3}{8}$	$1\frac{1}{2}$	$\frac{1}{8}$	4	3	3	$\frac{3}{4}$	$\frac{1}{2}$	$\frac{3}{8}$	$\frac{1}{4}$
Salinas City,	8	7	7	$\frac{3}{4}$	$1\frac{1}{2}$	$\frac{3}{8}$	$\frac{1}{4}$	8	8	1	$\frac{3}{4}$	$1\frac{1}{2}$	$\frac{3}{8}$	$\frac{1}{2}$
Todd's Valley,	8	7	6	$\frac{3}{4}$	$\frac{5}{8}$	$\frac{3}{8}$	$\frac{1}{4}$	7	6	1	$\frac{3}{4}$	$\frac{5}{8}$	$\frac{3}{8}$	$\frac{1}{4}$
Tomales,	5	4	3	$\frac{3}{4}$	$1\frac{1}{2}$	$\frac{3}{8}$	$\frac{1}{4}$	6	5	5	1	$\frac{3}{4}$	$\frac{1}{2}$	$\frac{3}{8}$

Tehama,	3/8	1/2	1/2	3/4	13	14	15		3/8	1/2	1	13	14	15			
Trinity Centre,	1	1	1	1¼	20	23	25		1	1	1½	20	23	25			
Telegraph City,	3/8	1½	3/4	1½	8	9	10		1/4	3/8	3/4	7	8	8			
Timbuctoo,	1/4	3/8	1/2	1	6	8	9		1/4	3/8	3/4	7	8	9			
Taylorsville,	3/4	1	1¼	1½	15	16	18		3/4	1	1½	15·16		18			
Tuolumne City,	3/8	1	1¼	1½	6	6	7		1/4	1	1½	4	4	5			
Ukiah,	3/8	1/2	3/4	1	10	11	12		3/8	5/8	3/4	8	9	10			
Unionville, Nev.	3/8	3/8	3/4	1½	20	23	25		1/2	1½	1½	20	23	25			
*Umatilla, W. T.	5/8	3/4	3/4	1½	7	7	8		1¼	1½	1½	6	7	8			
*Union, Or.	1¼	1¼	1¼	3	20	23	25		2	2¼	2¼	20	23	25			
Vandalia,	1¼	1½	1½	1½	16	17	18		1	1¼	1¼	16	17	18			
Vallejo,	3/4	3/8	1/2	3/4	2	2	3		1/2	1/2	3/8	1	2	2			
Vallecito,	1/4	1/2	5/8	3/4	10	11	12		3/8	1/2	3/4	8	9	10			
Volcano,	3/8	3/8	1/2	3/4	8	8	9		3/8	1/2	3/4	8	8	9			
*Victoria, B. C.	5/8	3/4	3/4	1	3	3	4		1/2	5/8	3/4	2	2	3			
Visalia,	3/4	1	1¼	1½	14	15	16·15		1/4	1	1¼	13	14	15			

GENERAL TARIFF—Continued.

OFFICES.	To and from San Francisco. Freight. Per lb. Under 50 lbs.	Over 50 lbs.	Over 100 lbs.	Treasure. Per cent. Over $100.	Over $300.	Over $500.	Over $1000.	To and from Sacramento. Freight. Per lb. Under 50 lbs.	Over 50 lbs.	Over 100 lbs.	Treasure. Per cent. Over $100.	Over $300.	Over $500.	Over $1000.
Vacaville,	6	5	4	¾	½	⅜	¼	6	5	4	3¼	½	⅜	¼
Virginia City, Nev.	8	7	6	1	¾	⅝	½	7	6	5	1	¾	⅝	½
*Vancouver, W. T.	3	2	2	1	1	¾	½	4	3	3	1	1	¾	⅝
Watsonville,	4	4	3	½	⅜	⅜	¼	5	4	4	¾	½	⅜	⅜
Woodbridge,	7	6	5	½	⅝	⅜	¼	7	6	5	¾	½	⅜	⅜
Windsor,	5	4	3	¾	½	⅜	¼	7	6	5	¾	½	⅜	⅜
Washoe, Nev.	8	7	6	1	¾	⅝	½	7	6	5	1	¾	⅝	½
Woodland,	5	4	4	½	⅜	¼	¼	5	4	4	½	⅜	¼	¼
*Walla Walla, W. T.	12	11	10	1½	1¼	1	¾	12	11	10	2	1¼	1	¾
*Wallula, W. T.	9	8	8	1½	1¼	1	¾	10	9	8	1½	1¼	1	¾

*Wilmington,	4	3	2	1	¾	⅝	½	5	4	3	1	1	¾	⅝
Woodside,	3	2	2	½	⅜	¼	⅛	4	3	3	¾	½	⅜	¼
Wadsworth, Nev.	5	4	4	1	¾	½	⅜	5	4	4	1	¾	½	⅜
Yreka,	30	29	28	2	1½	1½	1¼	30	29	28	2	1½	1½	1¼

WELLS, FARGO & CO'S
ATLANTIC AND EUROPEAN
EXPRESS.

Tariff of Reduced Rates from San Francisco to New York.

Photographs and Daguerrotypes:

In cases, usual size..................75c each
Letters, nominal value, Way Billed 50c "

Parcels and Packages—Not exceeding $25 in value—

Measuring 1-4 cubic foot and
   under, ...$1.00 to $1.50 each
Measuring not over 1-2 cubic foot 2.50 "
    "   " 1   "   4.00 "
    "   " 2   "   8.00 "

Intermediate sizes in proportion.

No parcel forwarded less than one dollar. Receipting for value over $25 and not exceeding $100, add from *one to two dollars* to the above rates.

Jewelry, Precious Stones and Valuables......................2 per cent.
Insurance.........................2   "

Gold Coin, Gold Bars and Placer Gold:

Sums under $500...................2 per cent.
Sums of $500 to $5,000.............1   "
Sums over $5,000...................¼   "
Insurance.........................1   "

Silver Bars:

Sums under $500..................2 per cent.
Sums of $500 to $10,000............1   "
Sums over $10,000..................¼   "
Insurance.........................1   "

United States Currency, Treasury Notes and Bonds:

Sums under $200.......$2
Sums of $ 200 to $ 300..1 per cent.
    "   300 to 1,000..1 per ct. on gold val.
    "   1,000 to 5,000..¾ " " " "
    "   5,000 to 10,000..½ " " " "
Sums over...... 10,000..¼ " " " "
Insurance.................1 " " " "

Freight and Insurance are payable at point of shipment, or on delivery, at shipper's option.

Freight on Parcels and Packages payable in U. S. Gold Coin on shipment, or if guaranteed, will be collected on delivery. Agents will be held responsible for the guarantee.

FAST FREIGHT.

Such as Boxes, Trunks and Bales (if in Bales at owners' risk) when measuring over two cubic feet will be taken at $2 50 per cubic foot, or 5½c per lb. When the weight of a package exceeds 45 lbs. per cubic foot, the rate will be per pound.

SLOW FREIGHT.

As above................$1.50 per cubic foot,
Or if by weight......... 3½c per lb.

Freight payable in U. S. Gold Coin on shipment.

Consignments to San Francisco are forwarded by WELLS, FARGO & COMPANY'S EXPRESS to all points on the Coasts of the Pacific and Atlantic, Sandwich Islands, Yokahama, Nagasaki, Shanghae, Hong Kong, European Ports, &c.

WELLS, FARGO & COMPANY'S
EUROPEAN EXPRESS,
FROM NEW YORK TO ALL POINTS IN EUROPE.

TARIFF OF RATES OF FREIGHT.

To all Points in England.—Small Parcels.

Photographs in cases, usual size,...$0.75 each.
Measuring ¼ cubic foot and under,.........................$1.00 to 1.50 "
" ¼ " and not over ½ cubic foot,..................... 2.50 "
" ½ " " 1 " .... 4.00 "
" 1 " " 2 " .... 6.00 "

PACKAGES.
Measuring from 2 to 5 cubic feet, additional per cubic foot,......................$1.00

SPECIAL RATES FOR LARGE SHIPMENTS.

To all Points in Scotland and Ireland.
Small Parcels additional per pound, (by Express)................................ .6 cents.
Packages " " ....3 "
Jewelry and Valuables, on value,................................1 to 2 per cent.
Insurance,..1 to 3 "

BONDS, STOCKS AND SPECIE.
Value $ 500 to $ 1,000, Freight 1 per cent., Insurance ¾ per cent.
" 1,000 to 5,000, " ¾ " " ⅝ "
" 5,000 to 10,000, " ½ " " ½ "
" 10,000 to 20,000, " ⅜ " " ⅜ "
" Over 20,000. " ¼ " " ¼ "
No Parcel forwarded for less than $2.00.

To all Points in Germany and Switzerland.—Small Parcels.
Photographs in cases, usual size,..$1 60 each.
Measuring not over ¼ cubic foot,.........................$1.50 to 2.00 "
" ¼ cubic foot, and not over ½ cubic foot,..................... 3.00 "
" ½ " " 1 " .... 5.00 "
" 1 " " 2 " .... 7.50 "

PACKAGES.
Measuring from 2 to 5 cubic feet, additional per cubic foot,......................$1.50
To all Points in BELGIUM, HOLLAND, DENMARK, SWEDEN and RUSSIA,
50 per cent. to the above rates.
Jewelry and Valuables, on value,................................1 to 3 per cent.
Insurance,..1 to 3 "

BONDS, STOCKS AND SPECIE.
Value $ 500 to $ 1,000, Freight 1 per cent., Insurance 1 per cent.
" 1,000 to 5,000, " ¾ " " ¾ "
" 5,000 to 10,000, " ⅝ " " ⅝ "
" 10,000 to 20,000, " ½ " " ½ "
" Over 20,000. " ⅜ " " ⅜ "
No Parcel forwarded for less than $2.00.

To all Points in France.—Small Parcels.
Measuring not over ¼ cubic foot,.........................$2.00 to 3.00 each.
" ¼ and not over ½ cubic foot,..................... 4.50 "
" ½ " " 1 " .... 6.75 "
" 1 " " 2 " .... 10.00 "

PACKAGES.
Measuring from 2 to 5 cubic feet, additional per cubic foot,......................$1.50
Jewelry and Valuables,................................2 to 2½ per cent.
Insurance,..1½ to 3 "

BONDS, STOCKS AND SPECIE, Same Rates as to Germany.

I

COTTON SAMPLES.

To LONDON, LIVERPOOL, MANCHESTER, and HAVRE, under 5 c. feet, $1.00 per c. f.
    "   "   "   " over 5 "   60 " "

HEAVY FREIGHTS.

Such as Boxes, Trunks, or Bales, when measuring over FIVE CUBIC FEET and sent
by Steamer:

To all parts of ENGLAND, IRELAND, SCOTLAND, WALES, etc., at rate of $1.00 per c. f.
To all parts of GERMANY, per German Steamer, at rate of............ 1.00 " "
Freight to LIVERPOOL, direct at.................................,..... 75 " "
  "   HAMBURG or BREMEN, at................................ 75 " "
  "   INTERIOR of FRANCE, North, at.... .... 2.00 " "
  "   "   "   South, at........................ 2.00 " "

EXCHANGE.

Drafts on DUBLIN, LONDON, LIVERPOOL, PARIS, and GERMANY, sent to Order,
on Remittance.

COMMISSIONS.

Articles of Clothing, Jewelry, Books, Instruments, etc., purchased on commission,
and delivered by Express in any Part of the United States. Commission
charged 5 per cent.

GENERAL DIRECTIONS.

Agents receiving Packages for us will please see that they are in good order,
and if they contain Valuables or Money, must be sealed, and the Value written
upon the outside plainly. On no account must LETTERS be inclosed inside
an express package, as it subjects us to a HEAVY FINE in Europe.

PETROLEUM and NAPTHA samples, CARTRIDGES or any goods
of a dangerous nature must *not* be received under any consideration, as these
shipments are prohibited by law under heavy penalties.

Agents will please inform parties sending, that the above charges for freight
DO NOT INCLUDE the CUSTOM FEE or DUTY; this is always EXTRA, and is charge-
able to parties receiving the packages in Europe, or if desired, can be paid by the
parties sending, by leaving a deposit of the PROBABLE amount with us. All
articles of value are dutiable, except into Great Britain, where they enter free.

*The above rates include freight from New York to destination. Express charges
to New York must be added.*

The LIVERPOOL Steamers sail TWICE every WEEK.
The FRENCH   "   "   ONCE   "   WEEK.
The GERMAN   "   "   FOUR TIMES every MONTH.

Heavy freight in quantities can be shipped direct to the different parts of Europe
at ONE HALF THE ABOVE PRICES for freight by SAIL VESSELS.

Packages containing samples, of no value, MUST BE PRE-PAID.

PACKAGES and FREIGHT should be marked distinctly to our care, or
sent under cover to our address.

WELLS, FARGO & CO.,

84 Broadway, New York.

TARIFF
BY WELLS, FARGO & CO.'S EXPRESS.

FROM SALT LAKE CITY.	On Money. Per Cent.	On Freight. Per pound.	REMARKS.
To Boise City.........Idaho.	1½	40	
" Bannock City........Mon.	1½	40	
" Benton.............Dak.	1	35	
" Cheyenne?.........Dak.	1½	40	
" Central City....... ..Col.	1½	45	
" Denver City.........Col.	1½	40	
" Fort Bridger.... ....Utah.	½	10	
" Fort Benton........Mon.	3	70	
" Georgetown..........Col.	1½	45	
" Helena ....Mon.	1½	50	
" Julesburg............Col.	1½	40	
" Kearney.............Neb.	1½	40	
" Omaha ....Neb.	1¼	40	
" Ogden......... .....Utah.	½	8	
" Virginia City ....Mon.	1½	40	

NOTE.—Discretion should be used in making charges on small packages and parcels, and where the article sent is not evidently worth the freight, pre-payment should be *demanded*. In all cases pre-payment should be *insisted upon*. To get the price to points on Overland Express, add to the rate to Salt Lake City the rate from Salt Lake City to destination. For points in the States, (to go Overland) add the rate from Salt Lake City to Omaha, and from Omaha to destination.

See Overland Express, Secs. 63 to 66, page

TARIFF
By UNITED STATES and AMERICAN EXPRESS COMPANIES to principal points in the States and Canadas.

FROM OMAHA.	On Money Per $1,000.	On Freight Per 100 lbs.	REMARKS.
To Albany.............N. Y.	3 00	8 00	
" Atlanta............ ..Ga.	5 00	13 75	
" Alton................Ill.	2 25	6 00	
" Atchison ....Kan.	2 25	5 50	
" Boston...... ....Mass.	3 25	8 75	
" Baltimore ....Md.	3 50	9 75	

TARIFF

By UNITED STATES and AMERICAN EXPRESS COMPANIES
to principal points in the States and Canadas,

(*Continued.*)

FROM OMAHA.	On Money Per $1,000.	On Freight Per 100 lbs.	REMARKS.
To Buffalo.............N. Y.	2 75	7 25	
" Burlington ....Vt.	3 50	9 00	
" Burlington ....Iowa.	2 50	6 50	
" Chicago ....Ill.	2 00	5 50	
" Cincinnati..........Ohio.	2 50	7 00	
" Cleveland ....Ohio.	2 50	6 75	
" Cairo ....Ill.	3 25	8 50	
" Concord.............N. H.	3 50	9 50	
" Charleston..........S. C.	5 50	14 25	
" Dunkirk............N. Y.	2 75	7 25	
" Detroit ....Mich.	2 25	6 50	
" Dubuque.... ......Iowa.	2 00	5 25	
" Des Moines ....Iowa.	1 00	2 50	
" Elmira...............N. Y.	3 00	8 25	
" Erie ....Pa.	2 75	7 25	
" Fort Wayne.........Ind.	2 50	6 75	
" Galena...............Ill.	2 00	5 25	
" Green Bay...........Wis.	2 50	7 00	
" Hartford ....Ct.	3 50	9 00	
" Harrisburg ....Pa.	3 50	9 25	
" Hamilton...........C. W.	2 25	6 50	Gold.
" Indianapolis ....Ind.	2 50	6 25	
" Iowa City...........Iowa.	2 25	5 75	
" Jefferson City........Mo.	2 50	7 00	
" Jeffersonville ....Ind.	2 50	6 75	
" Kalamazoo.........Mich.	2 25	6 50	
" Keokuk.............Iowa.	2 50	6 50	
" Kansas City..........Mo.	2 25	5 50	
" Lafayette............Ind.	2 50	6 75	
" Lowell..............Mass.	3 50	9 25	
" Leavenworth.........Kan.	2 25	5 50	
" Lexington ....Ky.	3 00	8 00	
" La Crosse............Wis.	3 00	7 50	
" Montpelier ....Vt.	3 50	9 50	
" Montreal.............C. E.	3 00	8 50	Gold.
" New-York...........N. Y.	3 00	8 25	
" New-Haven............Ct.	3 50	8 75	
" Philadelphia...........Pa.	3 50	9 00	
" Providence...........R. I.	3 50	9 00	
" Portland..............Me.	3 50	9 50	

TARIFF

By UNITED STATES and AMERICAN EXPRESS COMPANIES
TO PRINCIPAL POINTS IN THE STATES AND CANADAS,
(*Continued.*)

FROM **OMAHA.**	On Money Per $1,000.	On Freight Per 100 lbs.	REMARKS.
To Quebec..............C. E.	3,50	9 50	Gold.
" Richmond ....Va.	4 75	11 00	
" Raleigh.............N. C.	5 50	13 25	
" Rochester..........N. Y.	3 00	7 50	
" Springfield.........Mass.	3 25	8 75	
" Springfield ....Ill.	2 50	6 25	
" Springfield.............O.	2 75	7 25	
" St. Joseph...........Mo.	2 00	4 75	
" Suspension Bridge...N. Y.	2 75	7 25	
" Savannah.............Ga.	5 50	15 75	
" St. Louis.............Mo.	2 25	6 00	
" St. Paul...........Minn.	3 25	9 00	
" Troy................N. Y.	3 00	8 00	
" Toronto............C. W.	2 25	6 50	Gold
" Toledo ....O.	2 50	6 75	
" Utica.. ....N. Y.	3 00	7 75	
" Washington........D. C.	4 25	10 00	
" Winona ....Minn.	3 00	8 00	

NOTE.—In receiving packages for the above, as well as for all other points in the States, (Overland) Agents must require pre-payment of charges to destination, except on money packages. No package to be taken for less than $2 50.

www.ingramcontent.com/pod-product-compliance
Lightning Source LLC
Chambersburg PA
CBHW031243260626
47169CB00007B/2436